THE TABBART BRAND

D(wight) B(ennett) Newton is the author of a number of notable Western novels. Born in Kansas City, Missouri, Newton went on to complete work for a Master's degree in history at the University of Missouri. From the time he first discovered Max Brand in Street and Smith's *Western Story Magazine*, he knew he wanted to be an author of Western fiction. He began contributing Western stories and novelettes to the Red Circle group of Western pulp magazines published by Newsstand in the late 1930s. During the Second World War, Newton served in the US Army Engineers and fell in love with the central Oregon region when stationed there. He would later become a permanent resident of that state and Oregon frequently serves as the locale for many of his finest novels. As a client of the August Lenniger Literary Agency, Newton found that every time he switched publishers he was given a different byline by his agent. This complicated his visibility. Yet in notable novels from *Range Boss* (1949), the first original novel ever published in a modern paperback edition, through his impressive list of titles for the Double D series from Doubleday, *The Oregon Rifles*, *Crooked River Canyon*, and *Disaster Creek* among them, he produced a very special kind of Western story. What makes it so special is the combination of characters who seem real and about whom a reader comes to care a great deal and Newton's fundamental humanity, his realization early on (perhaps because of his study of history) that little that happened in the West was ever simple but rather made desperately complicated through the conjunction of numerous opposed forces working at cross purposes. Yet, through all of the turmoil on the frontier, a basic human decency did emerge. It was this which made the American frontier experience so profoundly unique and which produced many of the remarkable human beings to be found in the world of Newton's Western fiction.

THE TABBART BRAND

D. B. Newton

GUNSMOKE

This hardback edition 2010
by BBC Audiobooks Ltd
by arrangement with
Golden West Literary Agency

ISBN 978 1 408 46250 8

British Library Cataloguing in Publication Data available.

Printed and bound in Great Britain by
CPI Antony Rowe, Chippenham and Eastbourne

CHAPTER I

Sam Cochran was a blunt and forthright man, lacking perhaps in imagination but with a solid core to him. His character showed in the way he bore himself, in the direct look of sober black eyes and a seldom-smiling mouth. It showed just now in the way he bulled open the slatted door at McLeod's, moving like someone with a purpose.

There were no customers. At the bar, George McLeod had all the saloon's oil lamps lined up in front of him and was involved in filling reservoirs, trimming wicks and washing glass chimneys in a pan of soapy water. He wiped his hands dry on his apron and moved along the counter to a cleared place, as he nodded a greeting. "Beer?"

Sam considered, said, "I guess so." McLeod drew it and set it in front of his friend, first swabbing the spot with the bar rag. Sam put down his dime but made no move yet to drink. He said, coming right to the point, "I got your message. Archer didn't know what it was you wanted to see me about."

McLeod ran a palm over thinning sandy hair. "I hope I did right, sending for you. You'll be plenty busy these days, I know, with spring roundup to get ready for. But, this is about the kid."

"What about him? He isn't in trouble?"

"Well—I don't know. It could depend. . . . Did you know he was running with the Denkers?" McLeod saw the stabbing look Sam gave him across the lip of the beer mug. "No, I didn't reckon so."

Sam's honest face was dark. "How long?"

"A week or two maybe. They been in and out of here together, some. The first time I tried to drop a hint, knowing he was green to this part of the country and thinking I might warn him what he was letting himself get mixed up with; but

5

I had to go easy. Hell, I can't afford to have Floyd Denker busting up my place of business for me—maybe worse. And I figured the kid's old enough, he must have some idea what those devils are."

Sam nodded moodily. "Sure, George. He's of age." He worked at his beer, thoughtful and concerned.

"But then, after last night—"

"What about last night?"

"Well, Mitch come in acting pretty cocky—him and Floyd and Rupe, all three. I better tell you, the boy's run up a little tab for drinks; and I spoke to him about it. He suggested I touch you for the money but I said I wouldn't do that, I'd have to cut him off till he paid. Reckon, actually, I should have done it before. Anyway he got sore and begun telling me, one day soon he'd be able to buy me out and kick me out in the street. And then Rupe broke in on him, like he thought he'd said too much."

McLeod used his rag on the polished bar surface. "A little later, when I went around to their table collecting glasses—" He pointed with a nod of his bullet-shaped head. "—They quit talking the minute I got in earshot. But it was the way of it, more'n what I heard, that made me suspicious."

"What *did* you hear?" Sam prompted.

"Morg Osgood's name, for one thing." The saloonowner lifted his hands. "Look, Sam. Maybe I worry about nothing. Even supposing, let's say, that somebody's got an eye on some of that Clawhammer beef—hell, Osgood's plenty able to take care of the matter himself. What I don't like is the kid maybe being involved in it, with the likes of Uncle Rupe Denker. That really bothers me. Because I look on you as a good friend, it bothers me like the devil!"

"Thanks, George." Sam finished his beer. He set it down and stared at the empty glass. "Guess I should have managed to pay more attention. . . . Do you know where he stays?"

"I understand he's got a room at the hotel, shares it with a gambler named Boland. Boland sleeps days and the kid uses the room at night, so it works out cheap for them. But I wouldn't know where the boy is now. Ain't seen him at all, this morning."

"Uh huh." Sam made use of one of the row of hand

6

towels that hung from hooks on the front of the bar. "About that tab you mentioned. . . ."

The other man's face colored slightly. "Hell! I hope you don't think I was dunning you! It's only a couple of bucks. I'll get it from the kid."

But Sam fished up a black leather purse, unsnapped it and dug out a pair of crumpled bills which he smoothed out and laid on the counter. "That cover it?" Pocketing the purse, he said bluntly, "If the kid's not up to anything, then he probably hasn't got the money. Either way, I won't have my friends holding the sack. Just don't let him have any more credit."

"As you say," McLeod promised, and watched the other turn and take his big, solid shape out of there and into thin spring sunlight.

Standing on the saloon steps, Sam Cochran pulled off his sweat-stained hat and ran the fingers of one hand through a dark mane that glinted faintly with gray, even though he was a man not yet into his middle thirties—a stocky figure of a man, as serviceable and unspectacular as his jeans and denim jacket. The town dozed in the sun that was drawing tendrils of steam from ground turned dark by an early morning rain. The clouds had broken and drawn back to hang above the peaks rimming Colter Basin. There was the smell of spring, of new grass and rain-fresh sage and timber, and the tang of woodsmoke drifting from chimneys.

He pulled the hat back on again. His black horse stood tied at McLeod's hitch rail; he left it there. Waiting to let a freight wagon and team roll by on its way to the mercantile, he crossed behind it over wheel-rutted mud. The town, such as it was, lay scattered loosely the double length of this wide and rather shapeless street that formed its heart. A dozen business houses, three saloons, a couple of livery barns and the public corral with a blacksmith's shop adjoining, the sprawling two-story hotel: These were the essence of the place. A fringe of private dwellings along the side streets, with their backyard sheds and attendant outbuildings and a few pine and cottonwood scattered among them, spread out to meet the margin of sage and cloud-mottled bunchgrass.

That was the town. Sam Cochran liked it as well as any he knew.

Angling across Main, he mounted the wide steps to the

7

hotel veranda where a line of cane-seated rockers stood unoccupied in the sun. No one was behind the desk inside the lobby but the cheap ledger lay open, a stub of pencil tied to it by a cotton string. Sam ran a finger down the page, found what he wanted. Number Ten; upstairs front. He turned and traveled the worn linoleum and stolidly climbed the creaking flight of stairs.

At the door of Number Ten he paused with hand raised to knock, listening to what sounded like a faint sound of snoring. He rapped knuckles against the wood, waited and knocked again. But the person within seemed to be a sound sleeper, and the snoring continued uninterrupted. Sam tried the china knob. The door was unlocked; deliberately he shoved it open.

The room, with its faded garish wallpaper and dingy furnishings, was a mess. Clothing lay scattered about. A coat hung on the back of a chair, a flat-topped hat on a knob of the brass bed. A half-empty bottle of whisky stood on the dresser. There was a smell of booze, of cigar smoke and sweat. The drawn windowshade was a spiderweb pattern of cracks etched in bright sunlight.

Sam closed the door, walked over and ran the shade up, opening the window enough to let some of the fresh morning in. Afterward he turned to the bed, where a man lay sleeping in his long underwear, breathing noisily through his mouth. It took a good shake of a shoulder to bring him awake. Pale eyes in a ravaged, bitter face wavered open, came to a slow focus on the man standing over him. "Come on, damn it!" Sam Cochran said sharply. "Look alive."

The eyes darkened with awareness. Suddenly bedsprings squealed as the man twisted onto his side and shoved a groping hand beneath the pillow.

With surprising quickness Sam Cochran trapped the hand in a hard grip, and then himself reached under the pillow and brought out an ugly looking pocket gun—the kind that a professional gambler was apt to favor. His blunt features were hard as he released the man and stepped back. He tossed the gun onto the top of the scarred dresser; he had a gun strapped about his own middle—some instinct had warned him to put it on, when he received George McLeod's odd summons—but he made no move to draw it.

The man in the bed was up on one elbow, sullenly rub-

8

bing his wrist. His hands, like his face, were thin-fleshed, nearly colorless. He glared back at Sam. "What do you want?"

"Your name Boland?" The other nodded, and Sam suggested, "You know who I am?"

"I reckon. The kid pointed you out to me."

"Where is he?"

"Mitch?" Harv Boland scowled. "How would I know?"

"He's your partner, ain't he?"

"Partner? Hell, no! We trailed here together, but I mind my own business and so does he. I don't know where he is and I ain't seen him. Now, get out of here and let me alone!"

The gambler started to turn his back, to burrow down into the stale bedclothes again. At once, Sam Cochran's big hand descended on his shoulder and hauled him up—to a sit, this time, on the edge of the bed. "I'm talking to you!"

Pale eyes glared at him through uncombed, lank black hair. "Oh, hell!" the man said, finally. He ran the fingers of both hands through his hair, shoving it back. Then he got up, flinging aside the blankets, and padded in bare feet to the rocker where he got a pair of trousers and shoved his legs into them. He fastened them and thumbed the belt buckle in place. He turned to look at Sam defiantly. "Well?"

Sam crossed his arms and leaned his hips against the brass bedstead. "I won't waste time with you," he said, "because I got a feeling there's not much time to waste. Something's afoot—something involving my brother and Uncle Rupe Denker and I don't know who else. I got a notion you can tell me what it is. Likely you're mixed up in it yourself."

"Not a chance!" the gambler said quickly. "It's too tough a proposition for me to get involved in!"

"What is?" Sam prompted. Boland bit his lip. He had made a slip that time, and he was gambler enough to know it. The sallow cheeks colored faintly.

"You break into a man's room," he said belligerently, "drag him out of his own bed and start throwing tough talk at him before he's more than half awake! What the hell kind of answers do you expect, anyway?"

Sam stepped toward him and his arm came up with the same forward motion. The fist caught Boland square on the side of the jaw and sent him staggering; he fell into the rocker and it went over with him, putting him in a sprawl on the worn carpet. Sam righted the chair, picked the man up by the front of his underwear and dropped him into the seat. He stood over him, shaking the sting from the knuckles of his right hand.

"I expect true answers," he told the other man flatly. "And I'll get them—one way or another. I can bust your head for you if you insist on it."

Boland cringed, plainly expecting another blow. His pale stare shifted, chased about the room. He wet his lips. He jerked his head toward the whisky bottle atop the dresser. "You'll at least let me have a drink? I got to get the fur off my tongue. . . ."

Wordlessly Sam stepped and got the bottle, uncorked it and handed it to the man. He watched, stonyfaced, as Boland put it to his mouth and the muscles in the stringy throat worked convulsively. When he had counted five swallows Sam took the whisky away from him, palmed the cork home and put the bottle where he had got it.

"That ought to oil the works enough for now. Now, you tell me everything you know about this!"

The other rubbed a wrist across his mouth. He shrugged. "Why not? What do I care what happens to your stupid brother? Only, it won't do you any good." He squinted at the window, judging the hour. "What time is it? Pretty close to noon? Then I bet the show's already started. You haven't got a chance in hell of stopping it. . . ."

When he returned to where he had left his horse, Sam Cochran was a sober man. He wore the manner of one carrying a considerable burden, with nowhere to take it and no one to share it with. Certainly not the law—even if there was any closer than the county seat, nearly a hundred miles away. No, this was a matter that no one could handle but himself. And in fact, as Harv Boland had said, the chances were better than even he was too late and it was already out of hand.

Still, you could only try. Sam whipped loose the knot that had anchored his reins to George McLeod's tie rail, found the black's stirrup with his boot and swung up. A faint hope occurred to him, and he rode across the steaming mud and dropped off his saddle long enough to try the door of the

10

neat clapboard building that carried Doc Harnett's shingle. But the door was locked; and when it failed to open under his hand he somehow knew, beyond a doubt, that every word Boland told him had been confirmed.

His last hopes crumbled. As he stood there with head bowed and hand on the latch, Vern Tracy shoved his head out of his barber shop next door; razor in hand, he called, "Doc ain't in, Sam. He rode out somewhere, an hour ago. Dunno where to."

Sam nodded heavily, said, "Thanks."

The barber didn't like what he saw in the other's face. "Somebody sick, out at the Tabbarts'? Hope Jane and Leora's all right. God knows they've had all of that sort of thing they need!"

"Nobody's sick. They're fine," Sam told him, in a voice that left Tracy staring after him as he returned to his horse and rode on.

Free of the town, he had the entire Basin before him— actually a long trough, roughly oval, between folds of the granite-ribbed mountains. To the north it played out in a region of rough breaks; the southern half, most of it generally conceded to be Morgan Osgood's private domain, ended against a wall of lower hills. Good cattle country, rich in water and grass and timber, and busy now with the preliminary activity of a dozen spreads preparing for the big show of the cattle range—spring roundup. A moment's frowning debate, and Sam Cochran had decided the only thing open for him to do.

He set his course, and the black responded to the urgent touch of steel against its flanks.

CHAPTER II

An awkward man in some ways, Sam Cochran lost all trace of this when he had a horse under him; and the black was the favored mount in his string. It knew its rider's moods, and it almost seemed to sense the pressures that were bothering him now. Sam wanted speed, and the black gave it to him, following one or another of the many cattle trails that patterned the Basin rangeland. Sage and grass blurred past. Sam rode easily, settled well into the leather; he tried not to let his thoughts range too far ahead, or dwell on what he hoped to do when he got where he was going.

He passed Osgood headquarters at a distance of a couple miles, seeing the buildings as a distant spot of white against the tawny grass, and a flash of sunlight on windows. It fell away, swallowed up by a fold of hills, and leaving Sam just as glad not to have run into anyone who might have wanted to know what his business was. The ground began to lift and break now and he had to ease up on the horse, letting it rest for moments at a time while he chafed under the delay. When at last he came into timber, haste was out of the question.

Sam began to sweat a little.

Presently the game trail he had fallen into led him, laboring, up a long rise and through the cover of jackpine that crested it. He broke into the open at the edge of a shallow dropoff—and below him, saw a saddled horse, with its rider dismounted and waiting while the animal drank from a glinting meander of a creek. The horse was a strawberry roan, and the clumsy thing on its back was unmistakably a sidesaddle. The one who stood beside it, holding the reins, moved idly and Sam caught the flow of

12

full skirts; when she turned her head, the sun struck pale gold beneath the brim of the flat-topped hat.

Suddenly Sam Cochran was trembling a little, with relief and the quick release of long tensions. He blew out his cheeks. "I will be damned!" he breathed aloud. "Just maybe I'm in luck!"

He picked a way down. The tundra of the flat was spongy with the melting of snow that still remained, here and there, in shrunken patches. A million tiny frogs hopped and slithered away in front of the black's hoofs as Sam rode toward the woman, and the watery wire grass muffled his approach so that she didn't seem aware of his coming until he was a bare few yards away.

The roan lifted its head from drinking, then, and looked around; the woman turned, also. Sam saw her startled reaction, but she quickly disguised it. Her eyes were cool and her face expressionless as he halted his gelding and lifted a finger to hatbrim.

"Morning, Mrs. Osgood. Never meant to sneak up on you. Hope I didn't scare you any."

Sybil Osgood had quite recovered her poise, which was something she seldom lost. "Not at all," she said. "I heard you coming." She was handsome enough, Sam thought as he always did when he saw Morgan Osgood's wife. Though he didn't happen to know the word, her features would have been described as classic; and even in this land of strong winds and savage suns she had not let her complexion be flawed by weather. Her pale hair appeared to be lacquered, coiled and pinned beneath the hatbrim without a strand out of place. Sunlight, reflected off the rivulet at her feet, laid a tremulous sheen across her face and neat, full-bosomed figure.

Rumor had her at least twenty years younger than her husband; but then Morg Osgood was considerably more of a man, still, than some that were ten years his junior—which should make it about even. Anyway, Sam had always considered that this was Osgood's problem. His and his wife's.

She and Sam had never exchanged more than a dozen words, in the months since Osgood married and brought her here from wherever he found her. Now she was looking at

13

him with an expression he read as cool suspicion. She remarked, "You're rather far afield, aren't you? Mrs. Tabbart would hardly have business to bring you onto Clawhammer grass. . . ."

He didn't answer that. Instead he pointed out, "It's a remote piece of country for you to be riding alone, too, isn't it? I'm surprised Morg doesn't object. Of course, I guess Morg's not back yet from that Denver trip. . . ."

Her head lifted; her violet-colored eyes seemed to darken as she stared at this man in jeans and denim jacket and worn boots. "You sound almost as though you were appointing yourself my overseer! Really, Mr. Cochran!"

"Well—" he began lamely.

"I hope," she went on crisply, cutting him off, "you don't intend to tell my husband on me! He'll either laugh at you or be very angry; for it's simply none of your business, Mr. Cochran! Besides, as it happens I'm a very good horsewoman." She saw the look he gave the awkward-looking sidesaddle strapped to the roan mare and added, "Even if I don't care to ride astride like a common cowhand, the way that—the way some of your local women do!" At the last moment she had barely skirted calling Leora Tabbart by name, for which Sam had to be grateful though his mouth still hardened a trifle.

"I've ridden all my life," Sybil Osgood assured him. "We always had lots of horses, when I was a girl in Maryland and my father was alive. . . ." She didn't finish that, but the faint strain of bitterness in her tone was eloquent enough. Sam had heard that she had been rescued from a background of poor gentility, when Morg married her and brought her West to the Basin and the affluence of Clawhammer. "So," she added, "I assure you I'm perfectly capable of taking care of myself."

"Yes ma'am." He drew a breath, settling himself for what he knew he had to tell her. And then he stiffened as he saw, from the tail of an eye, the flash of brightness on a timbered ridge that made it unnecessary after all. He looked more closely, somehow remembering not to turn too openly to stare in that direction. He saw the flash again and knew it for what it was. He shifted his position in the saddle and picked his words with care.

"Maybe there's somebody ain't quite as sure as you

14

appear to be. Take a look—that ridge to our left, there just below the trees. You know anyone who totes a pair of field glasses on his saddle?"

"What!" The woman gasped and her head jerked, almost as though she had been slapped; all her coolness vanished. Her mouth formed an *O* and she turned swiftly to look.

"Come to think of it," Sam remarked, carefully watching her profile, "seems to me I've seen Grif Storrs use a glass, one time or another. . . ."

He couldn't quite tell what emotion he saw in the woman's face, at mention of her husband's foreman, but he decided it was anger. Her breast lifted on a drawn breath, within the smartly cut riding jacket; her lips closed and tightened. The fingers of one hand clenched and crumpled the dark material of her full riding skirt.

And then, as they stared again at the ridgetop, the shape of a rider and a horse eased briefly into view from the deceptive cover of the pines. It was too far to see the rider distinctly but no Westerner could ever be mistaken about a horse. Sam gave a grunt of satisfaction with his own guesswork.

"Storrs, all right. That's his sorrel, beyond any doubt. It's kind of flattering—a man as busy as he must be just now, with Morg gone. You don't suppose Morg told him to make sure nothing happened to you? But not to let you know they're worried about you riding alone—or guess you're being watched. . . ."

Sybil Osgood shot him a stabbing, naked look. "Oh, be quiet!"

Sam blinked and closed his mouth. And the woman, turning, got the toe of a polished boot into the stirrup and swung adeptly into the saddle, before he could think to make a move to help her. She settled her full skirt, lifted the reins. She looked again at Sam and her lips curled down, a disdainful set to them that somehow spoiled completely the handsome cast of her pure, patrician features.

"You," she said coldly, "haven't the slightest idea what you're talking about!" She kicked with a tiny spur, then, and the strawberry roan leaped under her. She took the jolt with a trained rider's grace, spun the animal on a dime, and a moment later was riding away from there—but in a direction, he was glad to see, that could only mean she had

15

called off her morning ride and was heading back the way she had come.

Sam Cochran let out his breath and it was a sigh of plain relief. He lifted a hand and with the knuckles of his thumb pushed the hat back on his head; the way it stuck to his forehead, he realized suddenly he had been sweating. That could have been much, much worse. He hadn't known how on earth to manage that scene, or how to tell the Osgood woman the facts of life as he'd learned them from Harv Boland. As it turned out, he hadn't needed to.

He looked again to yonder ridge. It was empty—the Clawhammer foreman had simply disappeared, taking his horse and his high-powered glasses with him. Whatever his purpose in spying on the boss's wife, he had unwittingly done Sam a favor; and the latter moved his lifted hand in a salute of thanks to the spot which he had vacated.

After that, knowing that only part of his chore had been accomplished, he pulled his hat down solidly again and spoke to the gelding. They took the meandering creek at an easy jump and rode on across wet and wiry tundra.

As Sybil Osgood brought her horse over the crest of a small barren hump, Grif Storrs broke from a stand of timber and came down off the skirt of the ridge where he had sat to use the glasses. Rather than seem to be avoiding him, she held her course. He hauled up, waiting; her face, as she rode toward him, was contained and nearly expressionless, only a faint tightening of her mouth showing the emotion within.

The foreman had pulled his mount athwart the trail and she had no choice but to draw rein. "What do you want?" she demanded, without preamble. Storrs took his time answering, heavy-lidded eyes appraising her. He was a lanky, rawboned figure of a man, narrowing from massive shoulders to the narrow hips of a horseman. A thick stand of blond hair, growing low on his forehead, topped a rugged face and a jaw like a shovel. The glasses swung in a leather case by a strap from his saddlehorn.

The woman repeated, on a note of rising anger that had just a shade of fear in it: "I said, what do you want with me?"

His black eyes were completely cold. "I've had more of you than I want, already! The day Morg brought you to this

16

country, I seen you was nothing but trouble—poison trouble. Clawhammer is a man's spread. There's no place for anyone like you on it!"

"That," Sybil Osgood said, "is not for you to decide."

He wagged his roughly chiseled head. "How damn well I know it!" he said bitterly. "A dozen years I've taken Morg Osgood's orders and never asked a question. If this is how he wants things now, I reckon I have to swallow it if it gags me!"

"Only good sense on your part," she told him, loftily. "It's been just as plain to me, since I first came, that there wasn't much likelihood of our ever being friends. Still, I see no point in being enemies—unless you insist on it."

"Anybody can have me for an enemy that does a thing to destroy this ranch!"

The ferocity in his craggy face startled and frightened her a little. "You can't believe I want that!"

"All I know," he said with dogged harshness, "while my boss is gone I aim to look out for his interests. And that means keeping tabs on his wife!"

She had a short, braided leather quirt; her hands, lying in her lap, tightened on it until the knuckles stood white beneath the skin and the nails scored her palms. "Why don't you call it by its real name! What you really mean is, you've been spying on me!"

"Call it that and see if I give a damn!" he answered, moving his heavy shoulders. His face took on a knowing leer. "You been doing a hell of a lot of riding lately, all by yourself—on that thing you call a rig!" He indicated the clumsy looking sidesaddle, with a contemptuous shove of his thumb. "I couldn't really believe you liked our scenery all that much, so today I decided I better be finding out just what you figured was so interesting. . . ."

Sudden fury and terror set her to trembling. All at once she was kicking her horse, driving it directly at Grif Storrs while the quirt in her hand lifted for a lashing stroke. She heard a sound that was like a bark of laughter, realized too late the foreman had only been goading her. He had better control of his horse than she; a single movement of his strong wrist reined its head aside, avoiding the frightened lunge of the mare. The braided-leather riding crop came whistling harmlessly down, missing him by inches. Her own

17

movement nearly spilled her off the saddle. She had to grab for a hold as the mare circled under her.

A hand closed upon her wrist, hard; a twisting motion sent sharp pain through her and dragged out a small scream of agony. Her fingers opened. The quirt was snatched from her and at once her arm was released.

Sybil Osgood stared. In Grif Storrs's rope-tough hand, the leather whip looked like a toy that he flipped and caught in his palm a time or two. As he looked at her white face, surrounded by a pale fog of hair that had come unpinned in that brief moment of struggle, his own face held an expression of such contempt that the words trembling on the woman's lips died unspoken.

The foreman said, "No damn female ever tried taking such a thing to me! I should use it on you instead!" But with a shrug he switched ends and extended the quirt's handle. She hesitated, reached and snatched it back again. Her breast lifted and fell with strangled breathing.

"I could have your job for this!"

"Oh, no you couldn't," Grif Storrs said calmly. "Morg would never be able to run this spread without me. I been his straw boss one hell of a lot longer than you're apt to be his wife—if you don't start watching your step!"

His mouth widened in a slow grin as he saw her face drain of color. She looked at him wildly; suddenly she kicked her roan into a wide circle around the foreman's horse and then let it out, along the trail back to Clawhammer. Grif Storrs twisted in the saddle and, for a long moment, stared after her.

With a shrug and a curse, then, he yanked his own animal around and followed at a more deliberate pace—herding Morg Osgood's wife toward home.

CHAPTER III

The building was a line shack, one that for some reason—judging by the shortage of discarded tin cans and other trash—was not much used these days but still appeared in good enough repair. There was glass in the window, the door hung true and the roof didn't seem to be missing any shingles. A feather of smoke wavered upward from the mud chimney, and a single horse—a big gray—was in a shed behind the cabin; otherwise Sam Cochran discovered no sign of occupancy though he rode all around it, carefully keeping to the trees that edged the clearing.

He saw no sign of violence, either, and he concluded that so far, at least, nothing alarming had happened. Making his decision, he got down and tied his horse back in the pines and then approached the house on foot. At the door he hesitated; the latch string was on the outside and he opened it and walked in.

The shack's single room was empty, but someone had been here. Pains had been taken; the floor was swept, the crude furniture tidied, the blankets smoothed on the bunk. The blaze of pine chunks in the fireplace greeted him with a fragrant warmth, and more wood was piled handily to renew it.

On the split pine table in the center of the room was something that struck an odd note—a black leather bag.

Sam walked over and picked that up, frowning. He knew what it was and who it belonged to; it confirmed the story Boland had told him, and he grimaced and set it down again. The fire was getting low, and almost without thinking, Sam went over and dropped fresh fuel onto it from the cut chunks of pine piled on the hearth. Straightening, he heard the door open behind him. He turned as a man entered.

19

Either John Harnett was older than he looked at a casual glance, or the graying of his temples and the lines that had come about his eyes and mouth were premature. Certainly he had the slim and erect carriage of youthful vigor and a young man's step. He entered the cabin, now, turning to close the door—a tall figure, broad shouldered in a well-cut town suit. The hand that swung the panel to and dropped the latch had a surgeon's strong and intelligent fingers; his face, in profile, was grave and sparely handsome. Sam looked at him and felt the contrast with his own rough-hewn shape, that was piled with blocky muscle and bluntly proportioned—a different sort of tool, altogether.

The doctor turned, then, and Sam saw that he carried a small bunch of early lupine, a dash of color that looked strange against the crudeness of the room; Sam wondered how far he'd had to go to find them. He came to the table, where a glass tumbler sat waiting. Pushing his doctor's bag to one side, he put the flowers into the tumbler. And then he went motionless as he saw, for the first time, that he wasn't alone.

After a silent moment Sam indicated the flowers as he said, "You better put water on those if you expect them to last."

The other man found his voice. "How long have you been here?"

"Just now walked in."

John Harnett's hands, resting on the table, tightened into fists and he leaned his weight on them. He needed an effort to keep his voice steady. "I wasn't expecting to find anyone."

"You weren't expecting *me,* at any rate," Sam interpreted. "I admit this end of the Basin is some distance off my normal range; but, I could say the same for you." He indicated the forgotten splash of color on the table in front of Harnett. "Those flowers, Doc: That was thoughtful, but I'm afraid it was a waste of time. She won't be coming."

He watched tides of feeling flood across the man's face, saw the color recede and leave the lean cheeks strangely mottled, the lines carved deep about the set mouth and narrowed eyes. "I don't know what you're talking about!"

"I think so. I'm talking about Morg Osgood's wife," Sam

20

answered bluntly. "I ran into her a while ago. We were talking and I caught sight of Grif Storrs watching her with field glasses—looking after Morgan's interests, I suppose, while his boss is away. When I pointed him out to her, she turned around and headed home."

"And sent *you*—?" The other man had dropped all shade of pretense, by now.

Sam shook his head. "I came on my own. You were never mentioned."

There was a moment while the doctor considered this, staring at Sam. The two of them were of a height, though they contrasted in every other way; they looked at each other across the table, in silence that was broken only by the crackle of the fire. Finally John Harnett straightened his shoulders and put into words the thought that made his gray eyes cold and dangerous.

"All right! Let's talk plain. Just what is it you want from me—blackmail?"

"Oh, hell!" cried Sam, and flung out a hand in an impatient gesture. "Is that honestly what you think? Blackmail!" He repeated the ugly word with a grimace. "I ought to just walk out on you! I'm here for your own good—yours and the woman's. And you'd better believe it, because there may not be too much time."

Harnett frowned in puzzlement. "What do you mean by that?"

"You know Rupe Denker?"

"I should. I've dug his bullets out of a couple of men."

"Then you know what kind of a tough, dangerous man he is—even if he is a cripple. Likewise, his nephew Floyd. . . ."

"But what could they possibly have to do with me?"

"Plenty! I just learned today that they know all about you and Sybil Osgood. They have a spy at Clawhammer, it seems—one of Morg's riders. I couldn't find out which. . . ."

"You mean, *they're* the ones think they can get blackmail? Out of a cowcountry doctor?" The other rapped the table with an angry blow of his knuckles. "By God, they're ripe for disillusionment!"

"It's you that keeps saying blackmail, Harnett," Sam patiently pointed out. "What they got in mind is something a sight bigger. According to what I heard, the plan is to take

21

Mrs. Osgood away from you, carry her off someplace and hold her a while. Until they can shake some kind of ransom out of Morg."

Harnett looked stunned; the color receded from his face. "Let them so much as lay a hand on her—"

"You'll do something?" Sam retorted. "You think you can scare Rupe Denker out of a thing once he's set his mind to it?" Sam shook his head. "I just don't think so! Today it didn't work because Grif Storrs scared Mrs. Osgood out of keeping her date with you. But there'll be another time— unless the two of you see that they never get the chance again."

The doctor's cheeks darkened with a slow crawl of anger. "Sybil Osgood and I are grown adults, Cochran; we'll make our own decisions, without any advice from you!" He added bluntly, "Anyhow, I still don't see who the devil invited you to stick your nose in!"

"I invited myself." Sam hesitated a moment, reluctantly decided he would have to tell the rest of it. "Happens I've got a personal reason. Sort of a family reason."

"Oh? What's that supposed to mean?" A sudden thought narrowed the doctor's eyes. "Wait a minute! There's been a young fellow in town, the last month or two. I've noticed him hanging around the bars, doing little of anything. And I heard somebody say you were related. . . ."

"We are. I hadn't seen my kid brother in years, until the day he showed up here; he's practically a stranger. Still, our folks being dead, I'm his only kin. I've made a few mistakes in my time; I can't just stand by and watch him pull some damn fool thing."

"Are you telling me he's involved in this deal?"

"That's what I heard. And that's why I figure I have to do what I can to stop it."

"I see." Frowning, Harnett rubbed the knuckles of a fist along his jaw. "Well, I think you're worrying too much. You know, you could have been misinformed. Or, maybe they've lost their nerve. Surely, they'd be here by now. . . ."

He was silenced by a suddenly lifted hand, as a sound of horses came down the wooded slope above the cabin. At once Sam Cochran, with a grim look on his face, was heading to throw open the door.

The riders came single file out of the timber; watching

from the doorway, Sam Cochran saw the full, bitter confirmation of what he had been told. Now he even knew the identity of the Clawhammer spy, for one of this quartet was an Osgood hand, one Sam had never liked—a man whose sun-bleached hair, sticking out like straw from below his sweat-blotched hat, had earned him the name of "Whitey" Yates.

And bringing up the end of the line was the one he had all along dreaded to see. A cold knot formed in his middle as he looked at the immature, too-wise face of his younger brother Mitchell.

He moved out into the open, then, with Harnett close at his heels. At sight of the pair the leader pulled rein so sharply that for a moment the rest bunched up behind him. Sam said coldly, "You people looking for somebody?"

Rupe Denker scowled as narrow eyes, pale and piercing, surveyed Sam over a bony beak of a nose. It would have been hard to say just how old a man he was. His hair and straggling beard were a dirty gray, his cheeks highboned and hollowed in deep grooves that bracketed a thin-lipped mouth. When he talked he revealed teeth too white and gums too red to be his own.

He had a gimp leg, from a crippling riding accident years before. He carried an octagonal-barreled Sharps rifle on his saddle, under one knee; and under the other, in a crudely fashioned leather scabbard, his wooden crutch. He was supposed to be a rancher, but everyone seemed to know that his shoestring layout in the North Basin was really a cover for brand-changing operations.

This spider of a man hunched in the saddle and peered from Sam to the doctor, beside him, and then at the door of the cabin they had left standing open. He looked puzzled and suspicious. Sam repeated his question, adding: "We're the only ones around. I'm afraid you've had your trouble for nothing."

The cheap china teeth gleamed whitely. "I dunno what the hell you're talking about, Cochran," the old man snapped. "But I certainly got no business with you."

"You certainly got no business with anyone else—not here, you ain't," Sam told him bluntly. "It's just not your day, Rupe."

Floyd Denker, who was twice the old man's size and

23

muscle-tough where his uncle was crafty, snorted and said, "He's talking riddles!"

"Is he?" John Harnett came forward, elbowing past Sam. "What is this story he's been telling me about you coming here with the idea of a kidnaping?"

Sam frowned, chagrined at having the play taken away from him, and their hand revealed before he was ready; but at least the results were positive. For a count of seconds he looked into vacant faces, at mouths that sagged in pure astonishment. And had there been doubt left in him, this moment settled it.

Big Floyd was first to find his tongue. "Where the hell you hear any such piece of nonsense?" he snorted. Suddenly suspicion flared in the muddy eyes, tightened the cheeks that held a shine of scar tissue gained in a hundred barroom brawls. "Why, I be damned!" he breathed, and his stare came around to nail Mitch Cochran's stunned features. "Didn't I say all along, this punk wasn't to be trusted? Didn't I? Just wait till I get my hands on—"

Mitch seemed to guess what was coming; frantically, he tried to pull his horse out of the way as Floyd lunged at him.

At once there was an angry roar from Uncle Rupe Denker: "Here! Here! Cut this out!" The homemade wooden crutch was jerked from its sling and, cursing viciously, the old man poked it at his nephew in an effort to fend him off. Floyd simply brushed the clumsy thing aside with an elbow. He was still maneuvering to reach the one he had called a traitor, when Sam Cochran finally managed to make himself heard.

"Let the kid alone. Damn it, it wasn't from him I learned about this!"

Everything stopped. Floyd Denker, twisting in the saddle, saw Sam's belt gun pointed squarely at him. His face drained of color and then, just as quickly, darkened with a rush of angry blood. But he held himself still as he demanded harshly, "Who, then?"

"It don't matter who. Just take my word for it—this little scheme of yours is finished. Sybil Osgood's not coming."

Old Rupe, still holding the crutch, let his pale stare narrow dangerously. "By damn! You warned her!"

"With the kid up to his neck in it? That's not likely!" Sam

24

retorted. "I never said a word about any of you. I didn't have to. She turned back of her own accord."

The old man seemed to believe this. He looked suddenly thoughtful as he slid the crutch back into its holder. Floyd, for his part, still glowered his fury. Sitting like a lump in the saddle, he told Sam, "You know what's good for you, you'll put up that gun!"

Sam shook his head. "I think I'll hang onto it a while. And maybe I'll ask you to set both hands on the saddlehorn, where I can watch them. . . ."

Floyd Denker looked a little wild, but he couldn't argue with a drawn sixgun. As though it cost him a real effort he lifted his big paws and placed them on the horn. They tightened there—the knuckles white, the wrists shaking.

Sam turned then to look at Whitey Yates. Yates tried to return his stare. After a moment, though, something seemed to happen to his eyes and quickly he, too, snatched his hands up and groped for the pommel of his rig. Sam said, in a tone of solid contempt, "And you're the one that set this up—by informing on your own boss's wife! Oh, I'd be proud, if I was you!"

"Go to hell!" But Yates's rejoinder was sullen, without fervor.

It was Rupe Denker who offered an argument. "After all these years of running Colter Basin," he observed, "to please his own damn self, I can't see why it should bother anyone to see Morg Osgood get took down a couple of pegs. Or his wife, either: Woman that'll run out on him when her man's back is turned—for the likes of *this*!" He indicated John Harnett with a scornful jerk of his head. The doctor chose to swallow the insult, returning nothing more than a cold look. When he got no answer from either man, the old range pirate lifted his stringy shoulders in a shrug. "Oh, well. Looks like all we're gettin' is nowhere. We might's well be riding."

"Just like that?" his nephew cried, in shocked protest. "Let ourselves be bluffed?" In his anger he lifted a hand away from the saddlehorn but the muzzle of Sam's gun stopped him and made him put it back. After that no one moved or spoke, during a moment while a gust of chill wind

25

came tearing through the trees and whipped at clothing and battered a pungent drift of woodsmoke among them, from the cabin chimney.

Old Rupe's stare held on Sam's face, pale and poisonous and speculative; his jaw waggled a little from side to side. He spoke, finally. "It ain't a bluff," he decided. "We'll ride."

"And how do we know these two will keep their mouths shut?" Floyd demanded.

"Don't be stupid! Is Cochran gonna turn the kid in? Is the doc gonna tell Morg Osgood he's been thick with his wife? No—they'll keep their mouths shut, all right!"

"They will if they know what's good for them!" Floyd muttered, a parting threat that he tried to enforce with a black warning stare; but in the face of Sam's gun it fell flat.

Old Rupe was already growling at his horse, pulling it around with a wrench at the reins. Whitey Yates, preparing to follow, had a hesitant look and a taut set to his mouth as he furtively sought Sam's eye. Sam knew what was troubling the renegade Osgood hand, but he wouldn't give any assurance that he meant to protect the man's guilty secret. There was nobody lower, in Sam's book, than the one who would betray the brand he rode for; he judged the range would be better off if fear of Morgan Osgood's finding out about today could somehow scare Yates into leaving it.

So, passing him up with a cold look, Sam turned to his brother as the latter picked up the reins. "Hold it, kid!" he said sharply. "Stay where you are. I'm not through with you, yet!"

Mitch, scowling uneasily, began a retort but bit it off. Nor did he get any help from the Denkers. Those two were not arguing any more with a gun; in another minute they were headed on their way back up the slope and into the trees. Mitch watched them go enviously, but he held his claybank down when it wanted to join the other horses.

Sam was holstering his gun when John Harnett seized him by the arm. "You let them off too easy!" the doctor cried.

Sam looked at him. "Any suggestions? Didn't the old man make it clear enough why there's nothing we can do?"

"I suppose so," the other said, and dropped his hand. "But—how do we know they aren't going to try this again?"

"If it worries you," Sam suggested coldly, "one thing you

26

can do is make sure they don't have another chance, like the one you almost gave them today. I suppose you know what I mean."

"Damn you, I said before—Sybil and I are adults. We'll manage our own affairs!"

"Then I hope you start managing them better!" Sam's temper was getting short, where this man was concerned. He saw muscles bunch under the skin of the smooth jaws. Abruptly Harnett turned and walked into the cabin, to emerge a moment later with his narrow-brimmed hat on his head and carrying his doctor's bag. With no further look at Sam he headed in the direction of the shed where his horse waited.

It was a simple truth, Sam thought, that he didn't know what to make of John Harnett. The man was intelligent, educated—a good enough doctor, and clearly Sam's superior in background and in a lot of other ways. How such a person could get himself involved with another man's wife was purely a riddle, to someone who liked to see things in simple patterns of right and wrong.

And yet, watching him walk away under the shifting pattern of sunlight and pine branches—slim and erect, in a city man's well-cut clothing—Sam thought he sensed an answer. The doc, and Sybil Osgood too, were of a separate breed and alien to the common style of life here on this west slope of the Colorado range. Though spoiled and discontented, Mrs. Osgood was a damned good-looking woman; she'd be attractive enough to someone educated enough to hold his own with her. By the same token, John Harnett would probably look good in contrast with bluff, unlettered Morgan Osgood. . . .

He shook his head. Cattle and weather and the many hardships of ranching this high-country region—these things he understood and could cope with; but human nature was too baffling and complex. And the biggest problem of all was waiting for him now, glaring defiance. He put John Harnett and the Osgood woman from his mind and turned to face his brother.

27

CHAPTER IV

He said, "Get down."

For a moment Mitch seemed ready to defy the order, but then he shrugged and swung a leg across and stepped out of the saddle, with graceful ease. "Go ahead," he said loudly, facing the older man. "I can guess what you're gonna say!"

"Can you?" A kind of dull defeat washed over Sam; he scrubbed a palm across his jaws. "Then you're some ahead of me! Damned if I can figure *what* to tell you, boy!"

"I hope you don't expect to keep me standing here all day, while you work it out!"

Sam eyed him solemnly. To an observer there would have been little resemblance between them. The younger man was slighter of build, lither, lacking the other's compact solidness. His features were more finegrained than Sam's, more likely what a woman would be apt to find attractive. His movements, and his thoughts, would be quicker but he was also more on the surface, suggesting lesser depths of character.

Even when they were boys, Sam had never felt that he really knew or understood this younger brother of his. Now years of separation had turned them into complete strangers. "Look, kid!" Sam exclaimed, making an effort. "I can't run your life and I don't want to—it's all I can do to manage my own. But at least I've been over the road; I'd like to try and ease the way for you a little."

"That sounds real great," the other retorted. "But when I come to this country hoping for a stake, would you give it to me? Like hell you would!"

"You know I didn't have the kind of money you were looking for. I'd have given you a riding job, at T Square; but that wasn't near good enough. That's not what you had in mind at all."

28

Mitch Cochran made an impatient gesture. "Your trouble is, you got no imagination. Look at you—at your age—still beating your brains out, punching somebody else's cows!"

"At least it's an honest living. I can tell you right now— you'll never get anywhere, running with the Denkers!"

Mitch's face tightened. "Now we get the lecture!"

"No." Sam lifted a hand and let it drop. He shook his head. "I got a habit of thinking of you as still a kid, like when we were all home and Ma and Pa were alive; when the fact is, you're grown and by now you *ought* at least to have a man's common sense. All the same it just ain't easy to stand back and not do what I can to help keep you from making a fool mistake. Hell, we're—we're *family!*"

"Yeah. And I bet you really hate it!" Mitch gritted between his teeth. "Here you are, holding down the best job you'll likely ever have—rodding a spread for a couple of women that figure they can't get along without you. Must make you real happy for me to show up and maybe do something that could blow it all out from under you! Well, I'm not leaving, big brother—not till I happen to be good and ready. Because, I don't like you much; and I don't really give a damn what you want. What do you think of that?"

Sam closed his eyes a moment. Almost a physical pain constrained his breathing. A sense of regret and failure engulfed him. He said heavily, "I think we're getting nowhere. We better quit this before one of us says something he'll really be sorry for!"

No answer at all, from Mitch. Sam turned and started walking toward the place where he had left his gelding tied at the edge of the trees. He pulled up once, looking around as he heard another horse break into motion. Mitch was in the saddle and spurring away from the clearing, following the direction the Denkers and Whitey Yates had taken. Sam watched him disappear into the trees, riding stiffly erect and not once looking back.

He stood there for a long time after silence had returned to the hills. Then, discouraged and sore of spirit, he went on to where the black stood waiting.

Roundup fever was something in the blood that hit the

29

range about this time of year. You caught it from the springing of the new grass, from the swelling of the creeks as drifts vanished under a warming sun, from the wavering wedges of geese that trailed northward filling the sky with their ghostly music. As time narrowed, every outfit in the Basin would be busy with a thousand and one essential chores, readying the day when they rode out onto the grass for the joint enterprise of gathering, branding, and tallying.

This year, for the first time, Sam Cochran in his sober and plodding manner carried the burden of T Square activities, alone. It meant full days for him and for the eight-man crew—checking riding stock and equipment, mending gear, testing each coil of rope and piece of leather on which a rider's life might in a crucial moment literally depend. The men liked Sam, knowing him for a good foreman who never made work just to keep his crew busy. He was not a boss you could joke with—he took his responsibilities too seriously for that—but he was fair in portioning out the work and if he kept a certain distance, they knew it was because his mind was full.

On Friday morning—almost at the last minute—he suddenly remembered a job that had not been seen to; he ordered Vic Bonner and Art James to tool the ranch wagon out of the barn and give it a going over, grease the wheels, and nail in place the homemade dropfront cabinet which converted the rig into a bedroll- and chuckwagon. While they got started at that job, he went to the cookshack to remind Smitty he should make out a list of needed supplies. Afterward, he was starting for the day corral when one of the hands brought word he was wanted at the house. He changed direction.

He saw as he approached the sprawling, log-and-fieldstone building how the line of cottonwoods behind it were budding out against a pale spring sky. Soon they would be in sun-flickering full leaf and drifting their cotton all over the place, the wind in the treeheads making a constant and pleasant accompaniment to the busy activity of a working ranch.

Sam liked this country, in all its seasons. It was a long, long time since he had felt a place was home, but he felt that way about T Square and the Basin. He would not have liked to think of leaving.

He knocked and entered the living room that stretched across the front of the house. Jane Tabbart looked around from where she was placing a vase, filled with purple iris, on the mantel of the deep stone fireplace; she said briefly, "Come in, Sam. Close the door." He pulled off his hat and stood waiting as she finished arranging the flowers to suit her.

Looking at them he found himself remembering those other flowers he had watched John Harnett bring into the line shack on Clawhammer, three days ago. More of the iris lay on the center table, together with the woman's coat and poke bonnet, and the thought occurred to Sam, She's been up on the hill. . . . There had been no flowers for Bob Tabbart's grave, that bleak day when they laid him in it last fall, and Sam knew it must have grieved her deeply. Now at last she would be making up for the lack.

She turned—a tall, proud woman, a good deal embittered by her husband's untimely death from pneumonia. Her gray-streaked hair was drawn back into a severe knot; the hands that smoothed her skirt were strong, work-roughened. She said abruptly, "How is the work coming?"

"Fair enough, ma'am. We'll be ready to move out with the others."

"I was just wondering what you've got the men doing with that wagon?"

Sam blinked. "Why, T Square has always sent out one of the roundup wagons for this Northern Division. . . ."

"T Square has always headed up this Division," she pointed out. "But it might not be so, now that Bob is gone. Have you heard any talk?"

"No, ma'am, I haven't. Except that Morgan Osgood finally got back from Denver yesterday. The organization meeting's tomorrow night. I suppose any discussion would come up then." These annual meetings, held just before the start of roundup, had become a matter of routine—of clarifying work schedules and coordinating target dates for the northern and southern halves of the Basin roundup.

Jane Tabbart said, "I could be wrong, but I have a feeling that Irv Paley's been resentful about taking orders from Bob these past five years. He may have it in his head to force a change, this time. He may want to try and run things, himself."

"You think so?" It was something that had never occurred to Sam. Considering it, he lifted the hand that held his hat, scratched his jaw with the thumbnail. "I'd kind of hate to see it—Irv's not too easy a man to get along with. But, I can understand how he might think he ought to have a turn."

From the tightening of the woman's tired face and the stiffening of her mouth, he knew that had been the wrong answer. "Is that how you look at it?" she asked, a little sharply. "Doesn't it bother you, to think of T Square being put into the second place?"

"Why, ma'am, I can't figure it would mean that," Sam argued, meeting her accusing look. "I always understood everyone was equal partners in the operation."

"I wonder," Jane Tabbart suggested a shade too quietly, "if the truth is you'd rather see someone else take charge of this roundup? That you don't really think you're capable? If that's it, I'd appreciate your being honest about it."

His head jerked. He felt the heat begin to rise from his throat into his cheeks as he tried to answer. And then they both turned, for Leora Tabbart was speaking from the hall doorway: "Not capable! Sam? Why, Mama, how can you say a thing like that? As though there could be any slightest reason to think it!"

Sam Cochran saw the way the older woman settled her shoulders, the prim set of exasperation that shaped her mouth. "I'm not saying it," she answered patiently. "Or thinking it either. I know he's always been most reliable, and a real help to your father."

"I should say he's been more than *that!*" Leora insisted, in indignation. She came into the room. She was tall, like her mother, but she'd had her good, clear-eyed features from Bob. Usually, as now, she favored a blouse and jeans, or at least a divided riding skirt. As she entered she was carrying her flat-crowned hat by its throat latch; light brown curls hung free to brush her shoulders as she looked quickly from one person to the other. "Why, when Papa lay dying, he said he could only bear leaving us because he knew he'd be leaving us Sam! You haven't forgotten already?"

"Of course I haven't forgotten." Jane made a small, irritated gesture. "And I really don't know what we're arguing about. We were discussing the meeting tomorrow

32

night; and something was said—I don't even remember what. It isn't important." She turned to the table, picked up her bonnet and coat and the rest of the flowers she had laid there.

Sam, looking at her and at Leora's troubled frown, felt that he had to say something. He cleared his throat. "It *is* important," he insisted. "I like my work and I try to earn my wages. Any time I might fail to, I'm not expecting a free ride; it's been enough of an honor that Bob Tabbart made me his foreman, and that you folks have kept me on.

"If it turns out the other outfits want me to boss this roundup, in Bob's place, I reckon I can do a job. Or, if it's to be Paley—or Red Steens, or whoever—I promise to see to it T Square will hold up its end."

Jane had stood and listened to this speech, her arms encumbered, her face without expression. Now she nodded and said, in her abrupt manner, "Thank you, Sam. That's all anyone asks." She glanced at her daughter, and brought an end to the scene by leaving the room—a proud, aging woman who moved with a quick full stride and head held high, as though to meet whatever blows could still be dealt her by a world that had taken her husband while in his prime.

Sam drew a breath and glanced at Leora. His hand was already on the doorknob when she exclaimed, "Sam! Wait!" and followed him outside, drawing the door closed as she faced him in the shadow of the porch. She spoke a little breathlessly:

"I do hope you understand. No one can really guess how hard Papa's going has been on her. Now that all she has is the ranch he built, her main concern is for it never to be any less than what he made it. You see, it's nothing at all against *you*, Sam."

"I know that," he said, nodding. "It's how I figured. Not being a man herself, she has to rely on someone else to run the spread for her—and whatever I am, I've had it pointed out to me that I'm no Bob Tabbart. Otherwise I'd be building my own spread now, instead of drawing wages. So I couldn't blame her, worrying about having to put faith in an unknown quantity like me."

The girl appeared to hear something in his voice that made her lay a hand on his sleeve. "I'm not worrying, Sam,"

33

Leora said earnestly. "And neither will she—just give her a little time. You're a good man; I've got all the confidence in the world in you. Whatever happens, you mustn't let anybody or anything make you lose your own!"

He stammered something; when he went back to work, it was as though he could still feel the touch of her hand on his arm. After all, Sam Cochran had been a little in love with this girl from the day he first arrived at T Square. He had watched her grow from a leggy colt into a beauty, with masses of taffy-colored hair and eyes so deep blue you felt you would lose your balance and fall in and drown in them.

There was a gap of seven years or so in their ages, of course, but the real void between them was a far vaster one than that. As a common puncher, and afterwards as top hand and even foreman—Sam had known the gulf separating ranch owner from someone on the payroll was almost beyond bridging. And yet, for just a moment, Leora Tabbart had reached across and touched him, not only physically but with the warmth of her friendship and her trust.

Even if Jane's doubts of him should prove true, and he some way failed this job that meant so much to him—it had been a moment he was never likely to forget.

CHAPTER V

The big meeting on Saturday night, just before start of roundup week, was always held in town since this was central to the Basin and convenient for everyone. It took place above Murphy's Store, in the room that served as council chamber for the village government and housed the annual Christmas dance and other such events. Tonight the men began arriving early—the dozen ranch owners of the Basin, mostly fetching along one or two of their top riders while the bulk of their crews headed for a final blast in the town's saloons.

A silver dinnerplate of a moon hung above the eastern rim, flooding the world with its glow and with a primitive poetry that acted strangely on these men: Despite the night-time chill of early spring it held them outside, a dark cluster of figures who gathered around the foot of the steps and smoked as they talked in hushed tones, exchanging laughs and range gossip. Roundup would be an old, old business before they were finished with it, but just now it was something to look forward to—a break in routine, an official end to the rigors and monotony of winter and the herald of a new season. . . .

Precisely at eight o'clock Morgan Osgood came along, trailing Grif Storrs and a couple others of his riders. This seemed to be the signal. Men rose at once from where they had been sitting; cigarettes were thrown away, a few respectful greetings were spoken. Osgood included them all in a brusque, "Evening, gentlemen. Shall we go up?" and almost without breaking stride started to climb the outside stairway, with the rest falling in behind him.

It was a few minutes later that T Square arrived, one of the hands driving Jane and Leora in the buckboard. Having

35

tied his black at a hitch post and sent the crew on, Sam Cochran escorted the Tabbart women up the steps. A hubbub of voices greeted them. Lamplight filled the room that held rows of hard wooden chairs arranged to face a table where Morg Osgood and a couple of other men were engaged in some last minute discussion. As these new arrivals entered, the sound of talk slowly died.

It was the first time in memory that any woman had attended a Basin roundup meeting; but with Bob Tabbart's passing, his widow and daughter were certainly entitled to fill his place. Red Steens came hurrying forward, lifting the hat he never removed indoors or out—a beanpole of a man with fading rusty hair, an old friend who solemnly took a hand of each woman, in turn, into both his own rope-scarred palms. Other men spoke greetings, even while staring—a little too openly, Sam Cochran thought—at Leora; it wasn't often they saw her like this, in skirts and petticoats, and he must admit the sight was uncommonly attractive. As Steens showed her and her mother to places in the front row, even Morgan Osgood rose part way from his chair behind the table, to nod once and then settle heavily back again.

In his middle fifties, solidly built, with a direct and incisive stare and a face that revealed few emotions except the truculent ones—such was Morgan Osgood. Such was the big man of Colter Basin, who by common understanding had the task of coordinating the Basin's annual roundup while taking personal direction of the Southern Division, himself. He laid both hands flat upon the table top now and his voice carried with authority through the room: "If we're all here, let's bring things to order."

That began a hurried search for seats. Those up front beside the Tabbart women were already taken, so Sam located one for himself in the back row. And as he took it, his eye happened to meet Irv Paley's and he gave a nod to this neighboring North Basin rancher.

The man merely looked at him coldly and turned his head away. At once Sam was reminded of Jane Tabbart's fear that Paley might have it in mind to make some challenge, tonight, against T Square's authority. The thought alarmed and sobered him. . . .

Morgan Osgood, about to speak, scowled instead and

36

looked at the door; for as the room quieted they could all hear indications from outside of more latecomers. Whoever it was they were strangely slow mounting the stair, the scuffle of boots punctuated at intervals by an odd thumping. Then everyone seemed to identify this, at the same moment. There was an exchange of looks, and someone cursed: "By God, don't tell me they've actually got the nerve—" In the next breath, the door was thrown wide and the Denkers entered.

Uncle Rupe Denker, humpshouldered as a vulture on that crude wooden crutch, halted in the doorway with big Floyd bulking massively behind him. He peered over the faces in the room, and the straggle of beard brushed his chest as he wagged his head.

"You owe me a drink," he announced, cocking a look at his nephew. "I told you there'd be a meetin' here tonight."

"Then why didn't nobody let us know?" Floyd muttered.

"Why, everybody's busy these days." Rupe's grin showed those china teeth, in all their improbable whiteness. "You know how it is, just before roundup. . . ."

Into the stillness, Morgan Osgood spoke on a note of infinite contempt. *"Get out!"*

The old man's head jerked; the grooved cheeks bunched as his pale glance sought the owner of Clawhammer. "What was that?" he shouted. If there was any fear or respect in him for the big man of Colter Basin, he gave no sign of it now as he went swinging, spider-like, toward Osgood's table—stumping deftly on his crutch, dragging the wreckage of a crippled leg. "Lemme hear you say that again!"

"I'll say it as often as you like! The decision was made a year ago: You Denkers are to have no further part in this operation."

The old man sucked in his breath. "Blackballed, by Gawd! Is that what you've done to us?"

Osgood shrugged. "You did it to yourselves—when you let us catch you putting your own brand on every slick calf that came under your rope."

"It's a lie!"

"Every man in this room knows different. By rights we should more than merely ban you from the roundup. Your kind oughtn't to be allowed in the Basin!"

"You think so, by Gawd!" And with a cry of rage the old man brought the hogleg up from his holster.

Sam Cochran's breath caught in his throat. Like himself the others at this meeting were unarmed, having left their guns at home or on their saddles. The Denkers held all the advantage; and for a moment Sam thought Rupe Denker actually had it in his head to send a bullet into the Clawhammer boss. Grif Storrs must have thought so too, for he straightened from the wall against which he had been leaning.

Quickly Floyd called a warning, as he raised his own revolver. "Uncle Rupe! *Watch it!*"

His uncle was already warned. Using that crutch with amazing agility he backed clear. Osgood's foreman checked himself as the sixshooter swung toward him. "You want this, maybe? Any of you?" The old range pirate turned to glance savagely about the room. He wagged his gaunt head. "You're a fine, sanctimonious lot of bastards—now that you got the whole range parceled out amongst you! Just as though none of you'd ever got careless with another man's beef, when it happened to suit your purpose. . . ."

Red Steens, in the front row, leaned forward in his chair and pointed a stabbing finger. "You are drunk," he said crisply, ignoring the menace of the gun. "And it's a plain insult, charging others with your own behavior. If you got good sense you'll leave—now!—and quit making yourself a nuisance."

"Maybe you'd enjoy," Uncle Rupe shouted, his face livid, "takin' an old crippled man and throwin' him down those stairs out there! Would you like that?" He hitched a step closer. "Well, I'll tell you now, mister—you'll play hell trying it! By Gawd, I'd—"

He broke off. His jaw sagged as, for the first time apparently, he took note of the two who sat next to Red Steens. The old man gaped at Leora Tabbart and her mother. "Why, ladies!" he exclaimed. "I purely never seen you, or I'd of watched my language better. Hope you ain't taken no offense at my careless way of expressin' myself!"

"It's not your language, Mister Denker," Jane Tabbart said in a voice that sounded prim and half-stifled with terror. "You could easily kill someone, the way you're handling that gun!"

"Yes, ma'am. I apologize." Chastened, he slid the weapon into its holster. "To you, too, Miss Leora. They may call him names, but one thing nobody ever said of poor old Uncle Rupe Denker—that he failed in showing proper regard to a member of the weaker sex!"

He lifted his head, as though expecting to be challenged on that; and thus he peered across the intervening rows and straight into the eyes of Sam Cochran.

Sam had somehow reached his feet, not knowing exactly when, but it must have been in the moment when he saw that pistol brandished so dangerously near to Leora's frightened face. Now he met the old cripple's stare and watched his expression shape itself into a malevolent caricature of a smile. Rupe Denker told the listening room: "Mister Cochran, there, and Morg Osgood and me—reckon that's one thing the three of us have got in common: We all of us respect a lady. Ain't that right, Cochran?" The man's whole face twisted up; one pale eye disappeared in a slow, conspiratorial wink.

Then, abruptly, Uncle Rupe was swinging away, clumping toward the door and waving his nephew ahead of him. "Come on, boy. We ain't wanted. Let 'em get on with their blackballing—see if we give a damn!"

Big Floyd wagged his head. "Reckon we got a few cards in our own deck, huh?" He waited, scowling furiously and letting the room see he still had his drawn gun, until old Rupe was through the door; then he backed out, in turn, ducking his head to clear the opening. The door slammed shut. Bootleather hit the outside stairway.

Immediately men were storming to their feet. A few even started for the door before they remembered they were unarmed and thought better of it. Somebody wanted to know, "What's the matter with this crowd? Didn't anyone in the whole damned room have a gun on him?"

"It was a peaceable meeting," Red Steens answered, his own voice trembling and face white with baffled anger. "And just as well, maybe. Somebody could have gotten hurt. . . ."

Sam heard bitter and blasphemous comment—that the Denkers should have been driven out of the Basin long ago; that they should have been strung up for brand blotting. Then Morg Osgood's voice was making itself heard and

39

Osgood's hard palm pounding the tabletop slowly brought order. "This is getting us nowhere," Osgood asserted flatly. "The Denkers are of no importance. If they dare to make any trouble for this roundup, they'll be taken care of— believe me. The thing now is to finish what we came for."

The temper of the room settled and they took their seats, though there still was some grumbling. Sam Cochran, at the back of the room, sensed a weight of questioning eyes and knew some of these men were puzzling over the last cryptic remark Rupe Denker had made to him. He saw Grif Storrs looking at him most oddly, and something in the Claw-hammer foreman's probing stare brought an unwonted tide of heat into his cheeks. The devil with him! he thought, and tried to put his mind on what Morgan Osgood was saying.

The Denkers had been no more than an interruption. He felt increasingly sure that the real explosion tonight was still ahead. . . .

For the moment, the meeting was back on the track and proceeding predictably. It had been a moderate winter, Morg Osgood reminded them, and preliminary surveys indicated there hadn't been too much drift south across Colter Creek, which divided the two halves of the Basin. Sometimes, in a bad year of blizzards riding a knife-sharp north wind, the beef of the northern ranchers tended to move massively ahead of the weather and collect at the lower end of Colter, as in the bottom of a sack; then it could be a devil's own job, needing every available man to help dig them out of the draws of the broken foothills and sort them and put them back on their own range. This time, presumably, each Division should be able to go ahead and complete its work independently of the other. Afterward, according to usual practice, reps from the North Basin outfits would be sent across the creek to help with the final cleanup.

Any questions so far? Osgood wanted to know, looking over the room. Any discussion?

"I got a question."

In the second row, Irv Paley hitched to his feet. He was a quarrelsome, always-scowling man, with thickets for brows and a heavy brush of mustache. One of his eyes had a slight cast in it, and the cheekbone looked as though it might have been broken in a fight and never mended properly. Everything he said tended to sound like a challenge. Now, bluntly, he announced, "Before we get into this any further, us North Basin men ain't chose a man, yet, to act as roundup boss in place of Bob Tabbart. Ain't it time we took care of that?"

Sam Cochran thought, bleakly, Here it is!

He could see Jane Tabbart's angry frown turned toward Paley. Beside her, Red Steens nodded solemnly and said, "Irv's right. It has to be settled."

"Very well." Morg Osgood looked over the group, seeking out the North Basin ranchers. "I'll give the floor to anyone who wants to offer a name."

He didn't get an answer, at once; they all seemed uncomfortable, each less than willing to be first to speak. As he saw this, Osgood's frown turned impatient. And then Irv Paley, still on his feet, set his jaw belligerently. "All right— I'll offer one, if there's nobody else of a mind to. The way it's been, we always let T Square have chief place in the Division because it run more beef, and put more riders in the field, than any other outfit north of the creek. But my Hat brand ain't such a damned poor second."

"Do I understand," Morgan Osgood interpreted, his look shrewdly probing, "that you're putting yourself up for the job?"

"I don't hear no objections," the man said, instantly on the defensive. "And I figure it's my right." He stared a challenge around the room, and Sam Cochran saw how these others turned away without meeting his eyes. Is he so dense, Sam asked himself, that he can't see how little anyone likes him—even if they're too good neighbors to say it?

Red Steens was the only one who spoke up, with evident reluctance. "I don't aim for a quarrel with Irv, or nothing," he said, his voice firming as he spoke. "But I for one always followed Bob Tabbart because I figured he was best for the job. And to my way of thinking the man he had working at his elbow, during those years, is the right one to replace him. To make this a horse race," and he got to his feet to do it, "I reckon I'll nominate Sam Cochran."

Sam blinked. He heard Irv Paley's outburst: *"Cochran! But—he ain't even an owner!"*

"What of it?" Red Steens retorted. "I'll take any man's

41

orders that I respect, and that I think knows which the hell way is straight up!"

The two cowmen stood and stared at each other, and the very air seemed to crackle; Irv Paley appeared, for once, speechless. Finally, into the heavy stillness, Morgan Osgood spoke and closed the matter: "Unless somebody's got some more names, I reckon we'd better put it to a vote. Maybe this had better be a secret ballot—and, of course, just the North Basin owners. When you've written the name of the man you want, Grif will collect them."

That meant a time of painful tension, prolonged by the need to borrow pages from tally books and pass pencil stubs around. Sam Cochran waited it out, hating every minute. At last seven ballots had been folded and deposited in Grif Storrs's hat, and at the table Morgan Osgood deliberately opened them, one by one, and placed them in a pile before him.

He lifted his head, finally. His eyes sought Paley's.

"Looks like you lost, friend. The vote is Sam Cochran."

No one moved, no one spoke. Then a ragged breath swelled the Hat rancher's chest. "You—you sure you never miscounted?"

It was the wrong thing to suggest. Osgood's mouth turned hard as he shoved the pile of ballots across the table. "Look for yourself," he snapped. "You got exactly one vote—your own, I imagine. You tell me how I could miscount *that*!"

All Sam Cochran could see of Paley's face was one ear, and he watched that grow slowly, painfully crimson. For his own part he knew he had won, likely enough, only because these people would not vote for Irv Paley. But however well he might do his job as boss of the Northern Division, he could be fairly sure already there was no point in looking for cooperation from the owner of Hat, or from his crew.

Then Morgan Osgood was speaking, giving Sam a summoning jerk of the head. "You're in this now, Cochran. We'll need to know your pleasure, concerning Monday morning.

"Step up here. . . ."

CHAPTER VI

It was no ordinary Saturday night. The last blowout before start of roundup was in full swing when Sam entered McLeod's and the noise hit him like a dash of cold water in the face, making him blink; stopping just inside the door, he had to pull his mind away from its preoccupation with what he had seen and heard and said in that room above the mercantile.

The saloon was crowded with men, its low, pressed-tin ceiling obscured by drifting tobacco smoke that swirled about the coal-oil lamps. Somewhere behind the din, the mechanical piano with its cymbals and bass drum attachment was pounding away without really being heard by anyone.

Red Steens and a couple other men who had been at the meeting hailed Sam as he entered, inviting him over to join them at the bar; he excused himself with a grin and a shake of the head, pointing toward the rear of the room to indicate he had business there. Already he was beginning to notice a change of attitude—people in the Basin had always appeared to like him well enough, but there was a new respect in their manner now that he had been officially named to head up the Northern Division. The thing that really impressed him, though, had been the smile of pleasure Leora Tabbart showed him—genuine pleasure, on Sam's own behalf, and not like her mother who was concerned chiefly with the image and prestige of T Square.

In any event, he was glad for both their sakes that he hadn't let them down. He felt a firm confidence about the roundup itself. He had learned the ropes under a good man; except for Irv Paley, he thought he would have no trouble from any of the men he would be working with.

43

As for Paley, the Hat owner was a problem he would face when he came to it.

Some of the T Square riders were in a group watching the play at a card table toward the back of the room, and he walked back there, coming up behind a young fellow named Jerry Brock. Sam laid a hand on the kid's shoulder.

"Hate to cut your fun short," he said as Jerry looked around. "But Jane and Leora are waiting to go home. Would you mind too much getting the team and the buckboard and picking them up?"

"That's all right," the puncher said. "I'd just as soon hang on to a little of my money." A grin flashed across his homely face. "Hey! I understand you're rodding the Northern Division. How 'bout that!" He punched Sam in the chest, a friendly gesture, and left.

One of the players at the table was staring at Sam with such hard intensity that the latter's glance seemed drawn to him, of its own accord. Above a fan of cards he looked into the eyes of the gambler, Harv Boland. Boland wasn't forgetting this man who had invaded his hotel room and pushed him around and forced information out of him. But Boland was the one who broke gaze, letting his stare waver and then slide away from Sam's to the spread of cards in his hand. And Sam turned his back on him and made his way through the crowd to the bar. He had more important things than a disgruntled gambler to think about, tonight.

His wellwishers insisted on buying him something to drink and he settled for a beer, working at it slowly and not taking much part in the conversation which turned now to the subject of the Denkers. It was just as well, Red Steens declared indignantly, that that pair had shown discretion enough to ride out of town before the meeting ended and they could be brought to task for what had happened there. He appealed to Sam: "What do you think? Will they try to make trouble?"

Sam picked his words carefully. "Hard to say. It was a pretty drastic move to blackball anyone from the roundup. I'd have voted against it. But I savvy your reasons and I'll abide by the majority decision. And, we'll keep an eye on them."

Somebody put into words what had probably been

bothering them all: "What the hell do you suppose the old bastard meant by that last remark he made—about you and him and Morg Osgood? Something to do with respecting a lady. . . ."

He looked into the beer mug he had just emptied. "Who knows what Rupe Denker means, by anything he says?" he grunted. But he was troubled by a recurring concern and, a moment later, he managed to catch George McLeod's eye long enough to draw him aside and put his question: "Have you seen the kid?"

"Mitch?" Perspiring with his labors, the saloonowner stopped to consider. "He hasn't been around much. Seems like I did notice him, earlier, but he must of took off."

With the Denkers, Sam supposed. There'd been small reason to hope anything he said to Mitch, that day at the line cabin, would change his habits, or awaken him to the dangers of the company he kept. He nodded thanks for McLeod's information, and left the saloon.

The white disk of the moon swam high, now, blanking out the stars in its vicinity and drenching the night with a glow that was nearly day-bright. Out on the street things were quiet enough, though the public corral and the hitch racks were lined with saddled horses. Groups of men occasionally clumped along the sidewalks. McLeod's pole was crowded and Sam had had to tie a half block further along the street. He went to his horse now, ducked under the pole and lifted the saddle fender to check the cinch before mounting.

Someone said, "Leaving?"

Osgood, with Grif Storrs and his pair of Clawhammer riders, had paused to watch him. Jerking the latigo, Sam acknowledged that he felt it was time to get home. "If I can have just a minute of your time," Morg Osgood said, "there's one more thing needs to be got straight."

"All right." Sam lowered the stirrup leather and came around the end of the tiepole, stepping up beside the others. "Where shall we talk?"

"Anywhere. It won't take long." Osgood looked about, saw the moon-filled niche between a couple of buildings. "Let's step in here." Sam and the rest followed him into the narrow passageway, out of the path of occasional traffic

45

along the sidewalk. Apparently satisfied, Osgood halted and turned. "As good a place as any," he said, and nodded to his foreman. "All right, Grif. . . ."

The first blow came without any warning, taking Sam full in the face and driving him, hard, against the building behind him. His skull rapped wood and the hat tumbled from his head. Astonished and momentarily dazed, he tried to turn and find the man who had hit him. His mouth held the sharp taste of blood.

"What—?"

Storrs's fist, with the weight of heavy shoulders behind it, took him high on the cheekbone. Stung, now, and angry, Sam overcame his first bewilderment and his own arms came up belatedly, in an instinctive move to protect himself from this senseless punishment. His shoulders slid along rough siding as he tried to fade away from the blows. Storrs waded forward, following him, but this time as he struck again Sam got a forearm in the way and managed, clumsily, to block it. And his own right fist chopped back, aimed at his attacker's face. He felt it land—not a good blow, but it knocked a grunt out of the man.

"Damn it!" Storrs said. *"Hold him!"*

Still unable to believe that this was happening, Sam tried to break clear but hands seized him; the two Clawhammer punchers, one on either side, had his arms at wrist and elbow and they slammed him back against the wall and steadied him there for Grif Storrs to work on. Hard knuckles took him just above the bridge of the nose, filling his head with an exploding of stars. A cheek was split by a glancing blow.

Flame spurted then as Morgan Osgood thumbed a match to life and put it to a cigar between his lips; between puffs at the cigar he said, "Leave his face alone."

So Storrs switched targets and sank a left into Sam's midsection, and a right that smashed against his ribs, above the heart. Gagging for breath, and with pain blooming inside his chest, the prisoner sagged on weakened knees. The hands continued to hold him, but as the blows drove home his head sank lower. At last a fist struck him on the ear and seemed enough to rip it from his skull. He was released; despite his best effort to stay on his feet he sagged limply forward, striking the ground with his knees and then dropping prone as his arms failed to catch him. He lay there dazed and retching.

After a moment he was turned over and his shoulders propped loosely against the side of the building. A hand seized him by the hair, lifting his face to the full flood of almost achingly bright moonlight. The black silhouette of Morgan Osgood showed above him. Osgood's rough voice said, as from a great distance, "All right, Cochran! This has been a taste of what you get, the next time you fail to keep your tomcatting on your own side of the creek. Do you understand me?"

Peering at the face above his own and trying hard to keep a grip on consciousness, Sam shook his head feebly against the fingers locked in his hair. "No. . . ."

The flat of a hand struck him across the face. Grif Storrs said harshly, "Damn it, I *saw* you. I saw you both! I knew she'd been spending more time alone in the saddle than she had any business doing; but with Morg away, Tuesday was the first chance I had to follow and see where the hell she went!"

Sam understood, then, the mistake that had been made. He heard Osgood saying, "Maybe you got some other explanation as to what you'd be doing on Clawhammer? Alone—with my wife?"

It was not a thing he could go into without dragging the whole sordid business of Mitch into the open, and he merely looked back at the man, unspeaking. After a moment, Osgood gave a grunt and the ruby glow of the cigar described an arc as he returned it to his mouth. Sam was freed and Osgood and Storrs straightened and backed away, to look down at him. The Clawhammer owner said coldly, "Remember, Cochran—you've been warned. There had better not be another time. Keep your mind on this roundup!"

He didn't try to answer. Boots scraped on alley cinders, then, fading in the direction of the street. He was alone with his hurts and with the heavy moonlight and intense shadows.

After a long time he pulled himself to his hands and knees, an effort that dragged a groan from him. Pawing at the building siding, he groped his way to a stand and leaned there, resting. The punishment he had taken about the middle made him fight to keep from retching, and he wondered if a rib might have been sprung or even cracked. The cuts on his face felt raw; when he touched his cheek he found blood.

Someone was hurrying toward him from the direction of the street; he heard his name, spoken anxiously. He lifted his head and saw John Harnett.

"This is terrible!" the doctor exclaimed. "I heard the whole thing. I thought I'd best wait until they were gone."

"Yes," Sam said heavily. "I bet you did!"

He pushed away from the wall, staggering a little before he got his weight steadied on his feet. He could breathe normally, he found, so he decided the rib wasn't broken. But when he tried to move toward the street and his waiting horse, Harnett was there in his way to lay a hand on his shoulder. "Man, you're hurt!"

"It's all right." He shrugged aside the hand. "Let me alone."

"The least I can do is take you to my office—make an examination. . . ."

Patience slipping, Sam looked into the shadowed face beside him. "Look!" he said bitterly. "I just took a whipping that by rights was yours. Now, if you got any sense at all you'll stay away from me! Clear away!" He added, "If you're so damned anxious to do something—hand me my hat."

"What? Oh—of course." Quickly Harnett found it and got it for him. Handing it over, he said in a tone of deep concern, "What do you suppose he's doing to *her?*"

Sam put on the hat. He thought of Sybil Osgood, with her elegant Eastern manner and her self assurance and her blonde good looks. He said coldly, "That's something you both ought to have thought of, at the beginning. But, I doubt if he'll do much. Whatever he might have in mind, I got a feeling she could talk him out of it!"

He turned his back on the man and made his painful way between the buildings, through the heavy moonlight, to the street. He almost felt as though he would need a ladder to reach the saddle of his horse. . . .

48

CHAPTER VII

Long before first light of Monday morning, activity began at T Square. Smitty had his fire going in the cookshack and was slamming pans around, making noise enough to wake the ranch. Soon lighted windows at the main house showed that Jane and Leora were up; and in the bunkroom, the crew was stirring.

Few men in the Basin were apt to be sleeping late, on this first day of roundup.

Through the partition of his cubicle at one end of the long bunkshack, Sam Cochran heard the murmur of voices and the creak of wooden bunk frames, and the thud of bare feet on rough boards. If anyone had an excuse for lying late abed at T Square this morning, it was certainly not the foreman; he gathered his courage and levered himself to a sitting position on the edge of the old iron bed. And then he clung there a moment with a hand pressed to his side, his lips tight clenched to keep any sound of pain breaking from them.

No question about it, he had a damaged rib—low, and on the left. How seriously Grif Storrs had hurt it with his sledging fists, whether it was splintered or only sprung, he had no way of knowing; he had been a fool, he supposed, to let pride refuse Harnett's offer of an examination. He had said nothing to anyone and had made a stab at bandaging it himself, pulling the cloth as tight as he could manage. The swathing of cloth helped somewhat, and he could get around; but a sudden move or even a deep breath caused a stabbing of pain.

Sunday had been a continual ordeal, yet so far there had been no comment from anyone and no questions. He knew, though, that everyone on the ranch must have noted the marks and swellings on his battered face. He'd been particularly aware of Jane Tabbart's disapproving look. She

49

must take it for granted her foreman had been involved in some Saturday night brawl, after the meeting in town; and she most certainly didn't approve. . . .

Closing his mind to the pain, Sam was on his feet and finished dressing as the clangor of breakfast call, beaten out on Smitty's dishpan, sent T Square's eight-man crew tramping noisily into the eat-shack.

This was the last meal any of them would be eating under a roof, for the next couple of weeks; and they did noisy justice to the mountains of flapjacks and the platters of fried eggs and bacon and mugs of coffee that were set in front of them. By the time they finished, leaving the cook to clean up the mess, the gray chill outside had a definite feel of dawn to it. In short order bedrolls were assembled, rolled and strapped and tossed into the wagon. Jerry Brock, the horse wrangler, had brought the cavvy in off night pasture and Sam gave the order to saddle up.

Without being asked, young Brock threw the foreman's tree onto his black for him; Sam was pleased not to have to wrestle the heavy rig into place himself. He was checking the cinch as Leora Tabbart came from the house, ready to ride—her mother didn't really approve of her dressing and working like a cowhand, the way Bob had taught her from a very early age; but Jane must have known better than to try and keep the girl at home on opening day, at least, of spring gather. Being Bob's daughter, Leora had a will of her own.

She paused now beside Sam, and as he straightened and turned to say good morning, he saw the quick look of concern cross her face. She must have sensed that all was not well with him, but Sam stubbornly refused to confirm her guess. He returned her greeting quietly, touching finger to hatbrim. Leora hesitated and then with a frown moved on.

Sam set his jaw, pulled himself into the saddle, and gave the order to move out. They went, with a whooping of excited cowhands and a brief pitching of fractious horses. Leora fell in at Sam's side, following the crew at an easier gait. The cook wagon, with Smitty handling the team, brought up the rear; while out on the grass, Jerry Brock and another hand looseherded the remount string.

Dust rose and settled on the line of cottonwoods behind

50

the house. A lamp still burned in an upstairs window; there, Jane Tabbart would be standing to watch her husband's crew pull away—leaving for the first time on roundup, without him.

It was still early when they arrived at rendezvous—a flat meadow toward the northern end of Colter, which always served as the collection point and cutting area for the first day's gather. The sun was just clear of the east rim, flooding the Basin with light and first warmth and raising a steam from the meadow creek's meanders. Red Steens and Tuck Edwards and their crews were here ahead of them; within another twenty minutes Jim Bowers and Ernie Raycraft came trailing in from their separate directions, and now it was beginning to look like a roundup—thirty men in the field, and a couple hundred head of horses being loose-herded on the grass. Smitty had his wagon unhitched and the wheels staked down, and a huge mountain of firewood had been gathered for him; blue smoke trailed from his fire, where the big graniteware pot was already brewing what would be the first of an endless supply of coffee.

The crews were in high spirits and anxious to hit saddle, but toning down their language and their horseplay in deference to Leora Tabbart. Though she made no special claims, as the only female in a bunch of men, not a one of them but was conscious at every moment of her presence. But she had long since proven she could hold her own on a cutting horse, with a rope or a branding iron; in her work clothes she was too much a part of the whole thing to inhibit them very much.

Presently Willis Harper and his three riders appeared, and now there were a half dozen outfits represented on the meadow. Harper had the longest distance of any to travel, his range lying far to the south, against Colter Creek, which was the dividing line across the middle of the Basin. After another quarter hour, Red Steens came over to where Sam and Leora were talking with some of the other owners. Steens was in a bad mood as he said, "All the brands are here but one. No sign of Irv Paley. Where the hell do you suppose he's at?"

Jim Bowers, a stooped, baldheaded man, said glumly, "If Harper could make it, then Irv's sure had plenty of time."

51

And Tuck Edwards added, "There's no reason he ain't here, unless to show what he thinks of us for not voting him in charge. Meanwhile, we're burning daylight!"

Leora looked at her foreman. "It's up to you, Sam."

Taking a breath—but not too deeply, because of the stab of pain from that rib—Sam Cochran made his decision. "I guess we'll have to start without him, though I hate to. . . . All right, Jim." He proceeded to give riding orders. "Why don't you take your crew and head up the Little Squaw and work that country below China Peak? Edwards, your boys and Ernie Raycraft's can swing east around Tyler Butte and come down Muledeer Creek. There's some rough country in there where the creek heads up but I think, together, you'll be able to comb it out." He went on, outlining the assignments for the first morning's work, receiving nods of agreement as each owner understood and accepted his job.

"I know that timber region under the east rim as well as anyone does, I guess," he concluded. "So I'll take T Square in there on Edwards's flank, and swing south toward the beaver ponds. That leaves the Fisher's Flats section for Paley, when he shows up. Everyone agreeable?"

Red Steens pointed out gruffly, "We named you to give the orders, Sam. You don't have to ask for approval."

It was a mild reproof, but Sam knew Steens's intentions were friendly. Before he could answer, a shout from one of the hands drew attention to the meadow's south edge; a new clot of riders was approaching, bringing another small band of horses and a second chuckwagon lumbering over the uneven terrain. "Hat!" said Jim Bowers, scowling. "They took their damned good time!"

Irv Paley rode up at the head of his six-man crew, astride a tough-jawed bay gelding that fought the bit and showed a quarrelsome temper very much like its rider's. Paley seemed not at all contrite at coming late. He reined in and wiped a fist across his thick mustache and demanded roughly, "Ain't this crowd ready to go to work?"

Resentment dripped in Red Steens's answer. "Now that you're here, Irv, I reckon we got permission."

The Hat owner seemed oblivious to his sarcasm. "Let's move, then. I figure we need a good outfit working the timber north of the ponds, so me and my boys elect to cover that section."

52

It was precisely the area Sam Cochran had named for his own crew, but he merely nodded. "All right, Irv, sounds sensible enough. Go ahead." Paley's stare, under the thickets of his brows, indicated he didn't care whether Sam approved or not. He was already turning his horse, with a yank at the reins that made the animal shake its head in protest.

As he drummed off across the grass, Jim Bowers started to exclaim, "Why, the bast—" but then changed the word as he remembered Leora Tabbart was listening. "You shouldn't let him get away with that! The man seems to think it's him that's running this operation, after all!"

Sam said quietly, "Oh, maybe not."

"I dunno, Sam!" Red Steens looked closely at the roundup boss. "He did countermand your orders! You could have made a mistake when you didn't call him on it—right then and there."

Sam felt acute discomfort but he held his ground. "I'll hear any man's suggestion, if it makes at least as good sense as my own. I figure I'd just as soon work the Flats, if he's got a preference. And I didn't want to pick a fight with him the first morning—for no better cause than that."

"But what about next time? And the next?"

"I'll try to take care of it when it comes. . . ."

The thing broke up then, as the owners went to call up their crews, take their saddles and scatter to begin the morning's work. Leora remained, and as Sam Cochran met her look her eyes were clouded, "Sam, do you think there's going to be trouble with Paley?"

He shook his head. "Reckon I can handle Paley. After all, the man has his pride, like everyone else."

"Everyone else isn't pigheaded!" she retorted. "What makes me feel guilty is that we're the ones put you into this situation."

"You didn't see me refuse the job, did you?" he pointed out, smiling.

"And disappoint Mother and me? Oh, Sam! If I thought, for a minute, you only took this on for us—"

"Don't worry about it," he assured her. "Maybe I kind of like trying to walk in Bob Tabbart's boots!" But he thought, as she walked away from him, that she didn't look entirely happy.

So began the Colter Basin roundup, falling into a pattern that would carry through with little variation, from day to day, for the whole two weeks: the mornings spent working a section of Basin range, bringing in the cattle that had become mingled and scrambled during the months since fall shipping; and then, afternoon chow, the process of cutting and separating the day's gather and tending to the branding of the calf drop.

These were days of endless toil, of swallowed dust and straining muscle, of the cursing of men and bawling of beef and squeal of horses, the smells of sweat and smoke and blood and burning hide. The cooks kept their fires up, with mulligan stew and coffee always ready when hungry men could grab time for a bite, while the wranglers roped fresh horses so that sweating, swearing punchers could switch their saddles from wornout mounts to others of their string and plunge again into the grueling labor. Slowly the separate cuts belonging to each Basin brand grew until they were large enough to be thrown over onto the owner's grass. And then, next day, move on to another section and begin the work anew.

At the heart of all this activity was the roundup boss, doing his own full share of the work while carrying the weight of all the rest—ready at any minute to settle an argument, to give the necessary orders or adjudicate the disputed reading of a brand. For Sam Cochran, that first Monday was the longest day of all, and the hardest; he thought it would never end. But it did, at last, and he stood aching in every bone and lifted a hand to return Leora's wave of farewell, as she rode away through early evening toward T Square—she might work alongside the crew all day, like any other puncher, but her mother enforced strict rules that would not countenance her staying in the field with them past sundown. Watching her disappear into the rim of pines, Sam tested that damaged rib with a cautious pressure of his hand. It hurt enough to make him wince; but by now he was convinced it couldn't possibly be broken, or he would never have been able to stand up through the day. So, that at least was encouraging—after a session in his blankets, he had a feeling tomorrow would see an improvement.

He was summoning the strength to unsaddle his horse

when Vic Bonner walked up leading his own bronc. Vic was a veteran T Square rider, with sharp blue eyes and a face like well-tanned leather, that crumpled into a different pattern of soft creases with every mobile change of expression. He peered shrewdly at his boss and said, "You look kind of peaked, Sam. You feeling all right?"

"Tired, is all," Sam assured him. "Like everyone else."

"You sure that's the extent of it?" But Bonner didn't press for an answer. He turned and called to the wrangler, young Jerry Brock: "Hey, Jere! Take care of these, will you?" The kid came hustling to get the horses; Sam and Bonner started for the wagon, moving stiffly on tired legs.

"A good first day," Vic Bonner said, as they looked across the meadow to where men and horses still moved about in the tail end of the day's work.

Sam nodded, admitting to himself that he was satisfied, except for the one small residue of anxiety represented by Irv Paley. A good beginning, a solid show of teamwork and accomplishment at the outset, always gave an extra jump and reduced the overwhelming appearance of the task to be done.

"Clouds building over the peaks, though," Bonner added, pointing with a jerk of the head. "We'll likely get some rain out of that." His dark, expressive face fell into folds of frowning apprehension; then he shrugged, philosophically. "Well, it'll settle the dust anyway."

"Sure." A grin eased the sober line of Sam Cochran's face. "Whoever heard of a roundup where everybody didn't end up wet, sooner or later?"

CHAPTER VIII

Actually the rain held off until the third day, and when it came it was the sort of drizzle that leaked from a porous sky and soaked into a man's clothes and turned the ground to greasy mud. The Basin men donned slickers, little hampered by the flapping yellow fishskins and the spill of water guttering from hatbrims. Sam Cochran felt it was little enough to complain of. The work was moving on schedule; Irv Paley, though scarcely civil, had made no further trouble. And, most encouraging of all, that sore rib seemed on the mend. He kept it bound tight but it gave hardly more than an occasional twinge.

It was on that third morning that Art James, a T Square puncher, was chousing a jag of a few head of beef down a wet, brush-choked draw, near the broken western edge of the Basin, when he heard a shout and saw big Floyd Denker on a rocky spur above him. In the rain, the man looked batlike and shapeless in a bulky rubber poncho. Floyd had a saddle gun, and when the T Square rider failed to heed his warning he whipped up the rifle and levered a shot at him.

It came close enough to set James's horse to pitching, while the steers ran ahead of him down the draw and scattered. His own belt gun was trapped underneath the yellow slicker and he did not feel like quarreling with a rifle. When he had the bronc settled he turned it and beat a cautious retreat, going instead to tell his boss.

Sam Cochran and Vic Bonner were together when James found them. They heard the puncher's story; Bonner swore and Sam, frowning, said, "You're sure you didn't do anything to rile him?"

"I was minding my own business, Sam. Didn't even know he was there till he yelled, and whatever he said the wind carried it away. After that he used his Winchester. And he used it like he meant it!"

Vic Bonner muttered darkly, "If them Denkers have declared war on the roundup, they've bit off too damn big of a chaw!"

Sam picked up the reins. "We'll go look into it. But keep your own gun in your holster, until we see just what's going on. . . ."

It was beginning to rain harder, with gray mists drowning the high peaks, and a wind that whipped in cutting lashes across a man's face—altogether the kind of weather that shortened tempers. James showed them the draw; it lay empty, the steers long since vanished, and no sign of a rifleman. Sam Cochran looked at the empty tumble of rock along the rim, where the rider pointed. He felt foolish, but angry too, as he shouted Floyd Denker's name and then listened and heard nothing but the slither of the rain.

Vic Bonner swore at a cold crawl of moisture down his collar. Sam tried one more time: "Denker, if you can hear me you'd better answer!"

Floyd's heavy voice spoke, from a wholly unexpected direction: "I hear you, Cochran!" And then the big man laughed as they all three jerked their heads about. The tube of the Winchester was pointed at them, and behind a slab of broken granite the shape in the black rubber poncho bulked darkly. Denker saw their consternation as they discovered they had been caught off guard, and he laughed again.

Vic Bonner couldn't hold back his anger. "What the hell do you think you're doing? Playing games?"

"You T Square riders are on grass where you don't belong," the big man called down to them. "Anything I choose to do about it, I'm in my rights!"

Sam Cochran took up the argument; it was hard to talk persuasively and reasonably when you had to shout every word into a rain-wet wind and with the barrel of a rifle looking down your throat, but he tried. "You know why we're here, Floyd. Interfere with us, and you Denkers will have the entire Basin to account to."

That got an obscenity from Floyd Denker. "You blackballed us from your goddamned roundup," he shouted back. "We can do the same."

Still seeking a sensible solution, Sam answered patiently, "Put away that rifle and come out in the open. We can't talk like this." And he urged his horse a step forward.

At once the rifle spoke, spitting a brief flash of fire and burst of powdersmoke that dissolved in needling rain. The bullet struck a yard in front of Sam, and Denker's challenge followed as the echoes of the shot went pulsing away. "Next time, by Gawd, I won't be shooting at the ground!"

Sam did not consider himself an extraordinarily brave man, but he was determined he shouldn't turn tail before the threat of that rifle. Mouth dry, and his grip on the reins tight enough that his fingers ached with cramp, he forced himself to hold his ground as he heard the snick of the lever jacking another shell under the firing pin. Afterward, careful not to touch the gun strapped under his slicker, he deliberately turned the black and rode to rejoin his companions.

Their faces held alarm and Art James stammered some angry question, which he didn't immediately answer. The two fell in with him and they kept going until they could pull up in the shelter of some trees where that rifle barrel would not be peering directly at them. Here Sam halted the retreat. Rain whispered in the branches and dripped about them.

Vic Bonner's dark face was cast in frowning lines. "I just don't get it! I think he's alone up there—and how can he expect to hold off the whole damned Basin singlehanded?"

Sam was following his own thought. "Do you know, I got a feeling there's something he doesn't want us to see. Why would he have picked this place to make a stand—unless Art nearly stumbled onto it, and he had to stop him somehow?"

"What do you think he could be hiding?"

"I don't know. I think I'll find out. You two hold him here—I don't care how you do it, but keep his attention while I do a little scouting."

He took Vic Bonner's anxious bid for caution with him— after all, even if they had Floyd Denker spotted they knew nothing as to the whereabouts of Uncle Rupe, to say nothing of the shady characters who from time to time holed up with them. The Denkers' end of the Basin was poor country—a chop of eroded draws and broken rock ledges, with only pockets of thin graze and a little scattered timber. A sizable number of beef, strayed from the better graze out on the open Basin floor, could easily lose themselves here, and to do a job it was essential that the roundup have an opportunity to search out its blind cuts and rugged coulees.

Sam didn't know what he was looking for, but he judged it must be somewhere beyond the point where Big Floyd had posted himself. He swung wide of that spot, riding blind; it was up-and-down travel, and despite the chill and the rain he was sweating a little when, all too often, he was unable to avoid skylining himself as he topped out of one of the eroded draws, or the scrambling hoofs of the black started loose rock to clattering. He could be thankful that, on such a day, there was no sun to pick flashing glints of brightness from his saddle trappings, and that sound was muffled by the rain and didn't carry.

Thus he was almost on them before he heard the mournful bleating of beef; it came from a deep draw whose upper end was so steeply enclosed that it was almost unscalable. Sam hesitated a long minute before trying it, but he had a feeling he had found what he was looking for. He saw what looked as though it might be a way down and he dismounted to try it on foot, leading the uneasy black on its reins. They came down without mishap, though the wet rocks were slippery. The sounds of cattle were louder.

Sam took to the saddle again, though as a precaution he unshipped his sixgun from the holster and held it across his lap, with the reins in his left hand. He sent his black on down the brush-choked, twisting throat of the draw, that had a tiny stream running through the center of it. The draw widened and deepened, the crowding sides and the brush fell back. A half-grown steer broke suddenly out of the growth and went bawling away ahead of him.

Moments later he found himself in a shallow pocket of grass and water, hemmed in by the rock walls; and there, some forty head of beef were penned—penned, literally, because as Sam rode slowly forward he saw that the lower end of the draw was closed off by a brush gate. He pulled rein and sat a moment looking around at the bunch of unbranded, slick-eared animals.

"So that's it!" he said under his breath.

It could only mean one thing, and Sam's face was bleak as he raised the hand that held his gun and rubbed the back of it across rain-wet cheeks and mouth. Then he settled his shoulders, knowing now what Floyd Denker was so anxious to keep secret.

Debating his best move, he rode as far as the fence to

59

have a look at its construction. It was built of poles and brush, and would be simple to tear down; but once that was done he knew he must be prepared for a fight. He didn't like to think of bringing the roundup crew here en masse and forcing a showdown, at gunpoint, yet this was a challenge that had to be met.

And then as he sat his saddle there beside the fence, the rain drizzling around him, a clatter of approaching hoofs jerked his head up. Suddenly Floyd Denker came spurring through the brush and dropping down across a shallow tongue of rock. His rifle was in his hand and as he saw Sam Cochran, past the barricade of the fence, the big man let out a shout of fury and he pointed the barrel of the Winchester at Sam and triggered in the same movement. The shot hammered among the rocks of the draw; the bullet itself went wide in its unaimed haste. Holding the lever Big Floyd simply flipped the weapon, to crank a new shell into the chamber, and then caught the stock beneath his arm as he came spurring straight ahead, readying for another shot.

By then Sam had remembered he held a sixshooter. He raised it, waiting deliberately for Floyd to get into good range. The slick wet rubber of Floyd's poncho filled his sights and he worked the trigger, feeling the buck of the weapon against his palm and instantly lowering the gun for a second shot if he needed it.

He didn't. The horse kept coming, but Floyd was about to lose his seat. He was leaning backward, being shaken like a half-filled sack of grain at each jump. His head began to flop loosely on his neck; his right arm swung wide and the rifle fell from it. And then he slid backward across the animal's rump and dropped, to strike the ground heavily and roll limply a time or two before he fell still, a motionless and formless heap inside a muddy poncho.

Slowly Sam lowered the gun to stare at this first man he had ever shot, while the echoes of the twin explosions slammed and bounced among the rocks. When he saw no movement, he let out a trapped breath from his lungs and afterward swung down—noticing as he did so that there was almost no twinge of pain, now, from the rib that had given him so much trouble only a day or so ago. Disengaging the fence, he led his horse through and over to the place where

60

Floyd lay; dropping the reins, he leaned and turned the big man over.

He wasn't dead—and seeing that, Sam's breathing came a good deal easier. He had aimed high, deliberately trying for the shoulder, and he saw now that his aim appeared to have been good. It was the sheer shock of the bullet that had knocked Big Floyd from the saddle.

He located a filled holster underneath the poncho and as a precaution transferred the pistol to his own belt, before putting his sixshooter away. He almost pulled it again a moment later as he caught the sound of more riders nearing; but when they broke into view he saw it was Bonner and Art James, who had heard the shots and were coming at a hurry to find out what they meant. They pulled up quickly at sight of Sam Cochran standing over his victim, and to Bonner's hasty question Sam shook his head. "He took it in the shoulder, knocked himself out when he lit. I think he'll be coming around in a minute."

Art James stammered, white faced, "He ditched the two of us some way. Must have got worried when he seen you'd disappeared on him. . . ."

Sam pointed to the fence, where they could see for themselves what he had discovered. Vic Bonner had a long look at the animals penned up in the draw, and he let out an angry grunt. "I'll be damned! No wonder he didn't want us to see what they been up to. Makin' mavericks!"

Sam nodded. It was an old range trick. You took a bunch of calves away from their mothers, who happened to carry a different brand from your own, and kept them penned up somewhere until they finally weaned themselves, and it was safe to put your iron on them and turn them loose again. These calves were big enough now, but as it turned out the Denkers had delayed a trifle too long about finishing the job.

If there was any question, Art James quickly dispelled it. He pointed out one of the animals in the pen. "Look yonder—an E R Connected. They caught up one of Ernie Raycraft's critters that was already branded, and never even looked close enough to notice!"

Vic Bonner's wrinkled face was wreathed in dark emotion. "What are we going do about this, Sam? And with him?" He indicated their prisoner, who still lay in the mud where Sam's bullet had dumped him though he showed signs of returning consciousness.

Sam had been asking himself that question, and he had his answer ready. "You two can handle the beef. There's no chance now, of course, of knowing who they belonged to except for this one in Ernie's brand; you'll just have to throw the rest into the maverick pool."

"And, Denker? I've seen places where men would be strung up for less than this!"

Sam's stubborn face was grim, but he determinedly shook his head. "He might be headed that way yet—and the old man, too. But I hope not, while I'm rodding this operation. I hope it doesn't have to come to anything quite that drastic.

"A bullet in his shoulder ought to slow him down, for the time being anyway. Meanwhile you do as you're told," he ordered. "Run that stuff back to the herd. I'll take care of Mr. Floyd Denker."

Bonner wanted to protest; even with a bullet in him, Denker was a skunk not to be trusted. But Sam would not argue and Vic had too keen a respect for authority to dispute a direct command.

By now Art James had already headed Floyd's horse and tied it to a bush. They pulled Denker out of the way and then the two crewmen took down the poles and piled brush that made the fence and went in and choused the mavericks out of there. Sam Cochran watched as they got them headed out of the draw and disappeared into the thinning mist that soon blotted up the sound of hoofs and the bawling of the cattle.

He turned back, then, to give full attention to his prisoner.

CHAPTER IX

He hunkered down beside the hurt man and, without too much gentleness, drew the poncho aside for a closer check of his wound. It didn't look too serious. The bullet had nicked his left arm, high toward the shoulder, but the bone was intact and the bleeding had largely stopped. Sam stripped off the man's neck cloth, ripped it in two for a crude bandage. As he finished, Floyd Denker, groggily awake now, cursed and tried to bat him away.

Sam sat back on his heels and watched calmly as the big fellow stirred himself and presently came up, swearing and groaning, to a sitting position in the wet and mud. Pain left him gasping. He clutched his arm and stared about wildly, and as his eyes lit on Sam the latter saw understanding darken them. "By Gawd!" he cried hoarsely. "*You* done this to me!"

"I most certainly did," Sam assured him crisply, and listened without expression to a further blistering outpour of abuse. When the man appeared to have run down he said calmly, "Now you got that out of your system, maybe you better see if you can make it into the saddle. I don't want to have to bother with taking you home."

"You can go to hell!" Big Floyd invited tersely. He sat a minute longer nursing his hurt, and after that came floundering to a stand.

He welcomed no help from Sam and the latter offered none, merely watching while Floyd stared about to locate his horse—and, in so doing, discovered the destruction of his fence and the missing beef. At that, the man's face grew ugly but he only stood looking in silence, for a long minute; then, without a word, he turned and tramped over to his horse. He whipped the rein ends free from the bush where they had been anchored and, moving awkwardly with his

63

left arm dangling motionless, hooked the saddlehorn and swung himself up.

"Want this?" Sam had found Denker's rifle. He cranked it dry, shoved it into the saddle boot. "And this. . . ." Having shaken the bullets out of Floyd's woodenhandled sixshooter he passed it up. Floyd accepted it without a word and scowling rammed it into its holster. Sam mounted his own horse and followed at a little distance as the man in the poncho rode ahead of him, out of the throat of the draw.

The rain had thinned and the clouds were beginning to break in dazzling streaks of light that patterned the overcast. Keeping an eye on Denker, it appeared to Sam that he was not any too sure of himself or of his seat in the leather. Floyd rode with head hanging, body giving to the sway of the horse which soon dropped into a walk and, after a moment, halted entirely. Sam shook his head, then, and took after him.

The man lifted a face that was gray with pain and beaded by sweat. "Get the hell away!" he muttered hoarsely but was unable to keep Sam from taking the reins away from him.

"Save your strength for hanging onto that saddle," Sam grunted, and waiting for no more argument he moved out ahead, leading Floyd's horse at trail.

Blue sky was showing and the sun glinted from only an occasional silver streak of rain when, at last, they came lagging into the yard at the Denkers' place. It was a miserable excuse for a ranch—a log house, in two sections, with a covered dogtrot separating bunkroom and kitchen. The shake roof sagged and had been patched raggedly with flattened tin cans; the rusted stovepipe stood at a crooked angle despite the guy wires that held it up. The ground roundabout was littered with rusting cans and broken bottles.

Approaching, Sam saw the corral and the three horses inside it. At sight of one of them, a bleak look settled over him; he was in short temper as he drew rein. The animal with Floyd Denker swaying drunkenly on its back came to a halt of its own accord.

In the same instant the kitchen door jerked open. With that surprising agility of his, Rupe Denker emerged swinging along on his crude, homemade crutch. A hogleg

64

pistol was strapped to his middle. Hatless, he stood with the damp wind ruffling his hair and straggling beard as he flung a fierce, appraising stare past Sam Cochran, to the rider of the second horse. His chest swelled on a sucked-in breath. He demanded harshly, "What's the matter with him? What have you done, Cochran?"

"I shot him."

Roused by the halting of his horse, Floyd Denker lifted his head now and saw he was home. He heaved his big bulk erect in the saddle, and then as Sam and his uncle watched he seemed to gather his strength and brought his thick right leg across his bronc's rump and swung heavily down, clinging to the horn and pulling his saddle so far over that the horse grunted and set its legs. Floyd turned, then, took a couple of unsure steps and went down flat in the steaming mud.

A sound of anxiety broke from old Rupe as he stared at his nephew. Turning his head, he yelled through the closed door of the kitchen: "Hey, in there! Kid, come out here—quick!"

The door opened. Mitch Cochran eased through it. He was gnawing at a chicken leg; when he saw the scene in the yard he tossed the bone aside and rubbed his palms nervously along his pantlegs, as he looked from Rupe Denker to his brother, and then to the prone figure of Big Floyd.

Uncle Rupe lifted his crutch and gave the young fellow a prod with it. "Well, don't stand there. Give him a hand!"

Something snapped in Sam Cochran, at that; he said harshly, "No, damn it! You don't have to. Don't touch him!"

Both their heads came up; their looks must have reflected something of the boil of anger they saw in his face, then. For Sam Cochran, this was suddenly more than he was ready to accept. He looked at his brother's blankly staring face and he said flatly, "Leave him where he is. Can't you see he's just a cheap, penny-ante cattle rustler? It's not fit for a Cochran to dirty his hands with him!"

That brought a roar from Uncle Rupe but Sam cut him off, saddle leather creaking under him as he swung back to tell the old man, "The big fellow isn't half as bad hurt as he thinks. It's a clean wound, didn't even bleed much; he can

65

take it in and let Doc Harnett look at it if he thinks he needs to. But as far as I'm concerned, he can lie where he is." He looked again at his brother. "As far as you're concerned, too, kid! You've had all you need of this outfit. Right now, you're coming with me."

The young man found his tongue. Stiffening he exclaimed, "Who says so?"

"I say so. You got any belongings in the house? Fetch 'em!"

Uncle Rupe squalled in fury and started to pull the sixshooter on his scrawny hip. But Sam had expected this and was ready for it, with his own gun in his hand and covering the old man. "Forget it, Rupe!" he snapped, his patience slipping. "Take that thing out of your holster and throw it into the yard—just so you won't be tempted!" Scowling thunderously, Rupe Denker nevertheless must have decided that even a patient and peaceful man, once roused, was better not trifled with. He was cautious enough as he lifted the weapon from the leather and tossed it a few feet from him.

Sam kept his own gun in his hand, covering Rupe and not unmindful of Floyd who, even though hurt and prone in the mud, could be tricky and dangerous. As he spoke he kept one eye on the big fellow, who was trying now to climb to his knees.

"You haven't bothered to ask why I shot him, Rupe; so I'll tell you: I found that draw and the batch of hand-raised mavericks you were holding, over east of here. He tried to stop me taking them."

The old man's face changed as he was speaking. The pale eyes turned flinthard and the cheeks sucked in against the store-bought teeth; but if Sam expected Uncle Rupe to protest his innocence, he was mistaken. The old man simply glared, and Sam continued: "Getting blackballed from the roundup doesn't seem to have taught you Denkers a thing. Just the same, you were warned that the Basin would stand for no more nonsense from you. Now I give you fair warning: I'm bringing my crew in here, and I'm combing every inch of this so-called ranch of yours. And I better not find any more of what I found this morning!"

Uncle Rupe raised a trembling fist. "By Gawd, you watch your step! This is our range! We're in our rights—"

"You got no rights! You forfeited them, along with those stolen calves. Still, it's the purpose of this roundup to protect every legitimate brand in the Basin; and that applies to yours, so far as it is one. But, you make one more move to interfere with us, and—well, just don't!"

He turned then to his brother. Still in this strange mood of angry assertiveness, he said curtly, "I'm not going to wait all day for *you*. Get your truck and your horse, and we'll move out of here!"

Mitch started to say something, checked it. He looked once at Uncle Rupe. Then he turned and walked past the old man and through the dogtrot into the bunkroom half of the house, coming out again a moment later wearing his gun and windbreaker, with his hat on his head and blanket roll over shoulder. Without a word he headed toward the openfaced tack shed.

Uncle Rupe could contain himself no longer. Pivoting on his crutch he shouted after the young fellow: "Damn it, boy! Hold on, now—"

"You shut up," Sam told him firmly.

Big Floyd had hauled himself to his feet. He stood swaying, clutching his arm through the folds of the poncho. He looked glassy-eyed, as though he might fall on his face again.

Now Mitch Cochran was coming from the corral, leading his claybank, the saddle on its back and the blanket roll strapped on behind. In silence he toed stirrup and swung astride. After that Sam gave the Denkers a final warning stare, and turned his black in a tight circle in the mud and slop of the yard. Not even looking to make certain Mitch would follow, he kicked his horse forward. Sure enough, as the ugly scar of the ranch layout fell behind there was the sound of a second horse following, and his brother pulled the claybank alongside of him.

They rode without speaking for a long and stretching period. Finally the younger brother blurted the question that was bothering him: "Was it really true, what you said back there? I mean, you couldn't have been mistaken? You got any real proof they were making mavericks?"

Sam answered, "Proof enough." He told briefly of the setup he had discovered. "It's too old a trick for anybody with any kind of range sense to miss," he finished, and add-

67

ed coldly, "I hope you realize I'm giving you the benefit of the doubt: I'm only taking it for granted you didn't have any part in it, yourself."

That stung a protest from the younger man. "Hell!" he exclaimed gruffly. "You must figure I'm really dumb, to think I'd risk my neck for the sake of a handful of mavericks—even if I'd known what was going on."

"I hadn't noticed you acting too long on brains," Sam retorted, "picking that pair for sidekicks! Well, maybe now you've learned something."

"Still trying to read me lectures?" Mitch pulled in, and Sam had to check his horse and turn back to face him. "In that case, I'm leaving you."

Sam shook his head. "No, you're not!"

His tone made the other blink. "What do you mean? You got nothing to say about me!"

"Oh, yes I have. I told you once before—we're family. I tried to wash my hands of you but I can't. Now, I'm doing something about it. Come along!"

"Where?" But he got no answer. Instead, Mitch looked into his brother's stubborn face and seemed to see something in the glint of the black eyes that stilled any thought of rebellion. He scowled, but he picked up the leathers. And they rode on together, in heavy silence, through a world made fresh by the recent rains, and polished to a sparkle by the returning of the sun.

At the holding grounds, the noon break was nearly finished and already men were catching up fresh horses to start cutting out the morning's gather. The tarps which had been erected above the cook fires were down, Sam noticed; evidently the roundup cooks believed the rains were over, for the time at least. Knowing Vic Bonner and Art James would have the rest stirred up and concerned over the outcome of the affair with the Denkers, he was for pressing forward but he pulled up a moment as Mitch demanded, with quickening suspicion, "What's the idea? What'd you go and bring me here for?"

Sam faced him. "What's it look like? I'm putting you to work."

"No! The hell you are!"

"Now, you listen! You've had your head and it's done

you no good; so maybe it's time I took over. We'll find out what a little honest labor can do. As of this minute," he added, riding right over his brother's protest, "you're working for the Tabbart brand. I'll pay you a cowpuncher's wages and, believe me, you'll earn them!"

Mitch Cochran's face was mottled; his voice shook with anger. "You can't make me! By God—I won't stay! I'll leave the minute you turn your back!"

"You do," Sam warned, not raising his voice, "you do and I'll come after you—and you'll wish you hadn't tried it! I mean that, boy—so, believe me, you might as well get it through your head: You're going to work this roundup, whether you like it or not. Any questions?" Getting nothing but a sultry, furious stare, he took it as settled and lifted the reins. "All right. Now, let's see if Smitty's got any grub left."

A surly, muffled comment: "I've eaten."

"I haven't. . . ." Sam Cochran seldom really lost his temper but suddenly anger was boiling through him. Leaning from the saddle, he brought the rein ends down smartly across the rump of his brother's horse. The claybank bunched and leaped forward with a suddenness that took its rider by surprise and whipped his head back and then forward again, with neck-popping force. Sam booted his own horse and they rode on that way into the busy activity of the camp at a good, dust-raising lope.

They were seen at once; Vic Bonner came spurring up from somewhere as they reached the Tabbart wagon, and his dark face held real concern. "Sam!" he exclaimed. "You all right?"

"Fine as frog's hair," the roundup boss said, pulling rein.

"We been worried as hell! I wanted to fetch up some of the boys, come back and make sure you hadn't run into—" He broke off as he got a better look at Sam's companion. Mitch returned a sullen stare, that included the handful of other men who stood about the fire, watching.

Sam explained shortly: "Got us a new hand. I dunno if you've met my brother Mitchell, but I've brought him to help out with T Square's end of the roundup."

"You two are related?" Sam saw the pure surprise reflected in the old puncher's wrinkled face and in the closer second look Vic Bonner gave the stranger. But whatever he might have seen or guessed, he asked no more questions than that. Instead there was a hint of quick, shrewd understanding in his nod.

"Good enough," he grunted. "We can always use another hand. Sure thing, Sam, we'll take care of him; we'll put the kid to work." He turned to Mitch with bland friendliness. "Son, you just come along with me. . . ."

For just a moment the boy hung back, and Sam felt drearily certain that he meant to make a scene. But something—perhaps the weight of all these strange eyes resting on him—must have discouraged him. Mitch Cochran appeared to settle a little more deeply into his own sullen aloofness; he favored Sam with a last bitter stare, holding a promise that matters between them were far from settled. Afterward, still not saying a word, he jerked the bridle and fell in beside Vic Bonner obediently enough. The two of them headed away in the direction of the herd.

Sam, swinging down, stood a moment watching them across his saddle. He felt very tired, suddenly, and very discouraged. He had no real hope that this experiment was going to work.

CHAPTER X

During roundup, a cowtown might just as well close up shop for all the business it did. For those two weeks, the crooked streets and the dingy, weathered buildings could belong to a ghost town. Everything marked time through the long spring days. Storekeepers took inventory, made up shipping orders, and then sat in the sun in front of their places of business, waiting.

Things stirred life only briefly, as on those rare occasions when a single rider from one of the camps came in off the grass with a list of supplies the cook needed, or to pick up the mail. Usually, when he did, he would put in at McLeod's for a quick drink before returning to his saddle and to the trails; and thus, without stirring from his chair behind the bar, George McLeod came to know as much as anyone in Colter Basin about the progress of roundup, the state of the range, and the clash and interplay of personalities out there in the field.

Alone at a table toward the rear of the shadowy barroom, Harv Boland spent the days. Usually the gambler had a glass in front of him, though he drank sparingly—rather, it was a way of conciliating George McLeod and keeping the saloonowner from ordering him out. He sat and with silent patience dealt poker hands, keeping in practice, and waiting like the rest of the town for the roundup crews to return with pay in their pockets, and life to pick up again.

"Or like a damned turkey buzzard," McLeod muttered a time or two, eyeing the man with chill dislike. He had little use for that breed, at its best; and Harv Boland looked to him like a tinhorn.

It was a restless time for John Harnett—even for him, business was slack. He stayed conscientiously close to his clapboard office in town, on call, well aware that bad accidents could happen on roundup and thinking, every time he heard a rider in the street outside, that it could be a summons for the doctor. So far the summons had never come. But on this quiet morning—a morning of sun and cloud-shadow, and of a still, insect-buzzing warmth that could have been borrowed from the summer that lay ahead —he heard hoofbeats approach and lag to a stop just outside his door. He laid aside *Pickwick,* that he had been trying from sheer boredom to track a stubborn way through, and getting to his feet walked to the door and flung it open. He stared.

This was no dusty, unshaven cowpuncher, smelling of horse sweat and tobacco. Instead, Sybil Osgood, mounted on her strawberry roan, sat her sidesaddle gracefully erect with the folds of a bottle green riding skirt arranged precisely; she nodded, her eyes cool, her face expressionless. "Good morning, Doctor," she said in a clear and impersonal voice.

His hand gripped the edge of the door; heart pounding as he looked hurriedly past the woman, he could see no one on the street—but it felt as though a hundred eyes must be watching them, as many ears listening to every word that was said. He swallowed and managed a reply: "Mrs. Osgood. . . . Is there anything wrong?"

"Oh, no," she answered politely. "Not at all. I'm well and so is my husband, as far as I know." And then, lowering her voice to a murmur: "I must see you! Now!"

His head jerked sharply. "No! That's impossible!" But there was an insistence in her look and he groaned inwardly. Another hurried glance along the street and then he said, with a lift of his shoulders, "All right. The trees above the bridge—in five minutes. But for God's sake, don't let anyone know!"

Not answering this at all, she simply tapped her mount's flank with the quirt she carried and moved on along the street without another glance. And John Harnett closed the door and leaned his shoulders against it. He was having trouble with his breathing.

This first stab of apprehension passing, he decided they could not likely have been overheard. He checked his appearance in the mirror, straightened his cravat and the

72

hang of his coat and got his hat from the wall peg. Leaving his office by the back door, he paused to check the blind rear of the row of buildings before he started away briskly, following a path through weeds down to the bank of Colter Creek, that ran behind the town at this point.

Here, beyond the reach of prying eyes, was a pleasant spot where the play of the creek mingled with a stir of wind in the heads of tall, red-barked pines. Harnett, arriving first, hurriedly scouted the place of the rendezvous and decided they would have it to themselves. This was a relief; he placed his back against a treetrunk and looked at the thousand scintillating flashes of sunlight dancing on sliding water, and waited. As the moments passed and his first concerned alarm began to ease, it was replaced by a growing, eager impatience.

A thud of hoofs muffled by pine needles brought him away from the tree, suddenly, to see Sybil riding toward him through the dappled pattern of sun and shade. Quickly he stepped to meet her. She leaned into his arms and he lifted her down from the saddle and then stood like that, breathing her name, unwilling to release her. The woman's violet eyes met his own coolly enough; but when he swept her close and found her mouth with his, her response was immediate, almost animal-like. Heated by it he trapped her lips a second time, bruisingly, until she moaned a protest and pushed against his chest to free herself.

This time, though reluctant, he let her go and she stepped quickly back. "My goodness!" she murmured, frowning a little, and put up a hand to touch her hair that his ardent embrace had threatened to disturb. The leather whip dangled from her wrist, by its thong.

John Harnett got his breathing under control; his fists clenched at his sides. "You know how you affect me," he said hoarsely. "Don't act so surprised!" And then he looked swiftly around and, as she started to turn away from him, caught her by an elbow. "You were careful, I hope?"

She winced slightly at his grip. "Why would anyone notice?"

"In this town, when a dog crosses the street they notice! Especially now with roundup going on, and nothing else to occupy them."

Sybil Osgood made a face. "It's just the same at

Clawhammer: This is the most boring time of the year—in the most boring place in the whole damned world!" She pulled away from him; her face was dark with petulance as she walked over to the edge of the bank and stood looking at the water.

The strawberry roan had lowered its head to graze, and the sound of strong teeth tearing at the grass was loud in the stillness. After a moment Harnett came behind the woman. He started to lay his hands on her shoulders, then let them fall without touching her. To the back of her golden head he asked, "Why did you want to see me?"

That brought her around to face him, her eyes hard and accusing. "I had to find out why *you* haven't wanted to!"

"You don't know what you're saying!" he cried. "This past week I've been in hell!"

"Have you?" she retorted, disbelieving. "Twice I've ridden up to the cabin. I thought at least I might find something—a message. . . ."

He stared. "You haven't gone back *there*? After what nearly happened?" He felt the sweat break out upon his palms. "Don't you know that Osgood is suspicious?"

"I don't believe it. He hasn't said anything to *me*. I haven't even laid eyes on him, since he took the field with his crew Monday morning."

"You mustn't let that fool you! He's suspicious, all right, and he's probably having you watched. Only thing, he thinks it was Sam Cochran you were seeing."

"Cochran!" Her expression was incredulous. "You're joking!"

"It's no joke. Grif Storrs saw you two together that day. And afterward Osgood had his men grab Cochran and give him a beating, within an inch of his life. I saw it!"

The woman's eyes hardened; her lips held no pity. "Serves him right, interfering in something that was none of his concern."

"He had his reasons," Harnett said, "but they're beside the point. The thing is, from now on we have got to be doubly careful. Every minute!"

"Because you're afraid of a beating?"

He flung out his hands. "Is that so terrible? I couldn't stand up to someone like Grif Storrs. I'd be a fool to try!"

"And so this is what it comes to!" she lashed back at him,

with scorn that whipped color into his face. "You're *afraid* of them, afraid even to see me again—until I finally have to hunt you out and force you to admit it!"

For a long moment John Harnett stood and endured the blaze of hurt anger, while he tried to find some answer that would not be an admission she was right. Finally, giving it up, he said in a voice that shook slightly, "In God's name, what do you want me to *do*?"

She answered at once: "Take me away from here!"

"Far enough that Morgan Osgood couldn't find us?" he exclaimed. "On the kind of money I could raise? Impossible!"

"You could find a way, if you care for me half as much as you say you do."

He was starting to protest when they both were startled by the boom of iron shoes striking loose planking. Intent on their own affairs, they had failed to notice a horseman approaching the wooden bridge that crossed the creek some fifteen yards downstream from where they stood. A rider was coming into town from the North Basin road, at an easy canter. It was already too late to break for cover; and Harnett flung an arm about the woman's shoulders and they stood motionless, pressed close together, until at last the trees and brush swallowed the rider up.

John Harnett released a trapped breath. His pulse, that seemed almost to have stopped, began to pound again and all his joints felt weakened. He could feel the woman trembling against him. "Who—who was it?"

"Couldn't make him out. A hand from one of the North Basin outfits, I suppose."

"Do you think he saw us?"

"We'll hope not. In any event, you'd better go!"

He moved to escort her to her horse, but she was not ready and she stood firm. She caught at the lapels of his coat and forced him to look at her; though still pale from her start, her face held determination. She said fiercely, "This matter isn't settled! I'll be at the cabin two days from now—don't worry, I'll make certain no one follows me. And I'll wait till you come."

His hands clenched, then opened again. Slowly he nodded. "All right," he said, and it was almost a groan.

Satisfied, she turned away at once, eluding his arms when

75

he tried to take her in a final embrace. He helped her onto the saddle, where she arranged her skirt and caught up the reins. Then, without a parting kiss or even so much as a word, she gave the roan a flick of the quirt and sent it forward.

John Harnett stood, a troubled man, and watched her ride away from him into the creekbank timber.

CHAPTER XI

It had been something like desperation made Sam Cochran drag his brother Mitch back to the roundup camp with him and forcibly put him to work. He felt no real hope of results. He had enough on his hands already, and in Mitch he could be saddling himself with another bad one—at the very least, a non-cooperative troublemaker; at the worst, a defiant rebel.

That first day went badly. Mitch seemed to be biding his time, making only the barest pretense of carrying out the tasks assigned him. Next morning Sam fully expected to find him gone during the night; yet surprisingly he was still there, wrapped in his blankets, asleep. Morning came at an early hour but Mitch rolled out at the summons of Smitty's breakfast call. He returned Sam's greeting with a cold stare; later, however, Sam was surprised to see him talking pleasantly enough to some of the other hands.

No question about it, he possessed a real charm when he cared to use it. It was for his brother that he reserved the full weight of his sullen hostility. He took his orders but he would say nothing in return, and he met any approach from Sam with a smoldering look that was meant to put him in his place. But, at least, he stayed.

Perhaps he knew that if he sneaked out, Sam meant literally what he'd said about coming after him and dragging him back; the humiliation of that was possibly more than he wanted to risk. On the other hand, there might be something more to it than that.

Mitch had always been a good horseman, even as a kid; he was strong and quick, with sharp reflexes; put a well-trained cutting horse under him and he could work a herd with the best of them, and he was a wizard with a rope. Everything seemed to come easily and effortlessly for him.

77

Now, Sam actually began to suspect the boy was enjoying this first real job of work he'd undertaken in no telling how long a time—and however he might resent being forced to do it.

At least Sam decided to be thankful that Mitch was out from under the influence of the Denkers, for the time being. This much was to the good, even if it made things personally unpleasant for Sam Cochran.

He had paused for a moment to observe Mitch working with the T Square calf branders, that second afternoon, when Leora Tabbart rode up beside him. Leora had been busy with ranch chores and had not made it out to roundup camp for a couple of days; now as they sat their saddles discussing the progress of things, her eye was drawn inevitably to the slim young fellow on the claybank who was helping bring calf critters to the fire. "Why, that's not one of our crew, is it?" she exclaimed. "Whoever he is, he's good!"

They watched him cut a calf away from its mother, deftly rope it by the heels and stretch it out for the branders and earmarkers to do their job. There was the stench of burning hair and the bawling of pain and fear; Mitch flipped his rope free, laughing at something. His teeth made a white slash across the lean darkness of his face. The grin vanished instantly when he heard Sam call his name, but he rode over, a mere nudge of his knee swinging the claybank while he deftly hauled in his yellow rope and coiled it.

The sullen submissiveness of his expression changed to something else again upon sight of his brother's companion. Leora, for her part, looked at Sam in astonishment as the latter made the introductions. "Why, I never even knew you *had* a brother!"

"Yeah, I can bet you didn't," Mitch commented, with a wicked glance at Sam who frowned, coloring slightly.

Sam told the girl, "I was surprised, myself, when he showed up out of nowhere. He and I had been out of touch for years. Still, we can always use an extra hand at roundup; I took the liberty of putting him on the payroll."

"But surely he'll stay on, after roundup's over?"

Mitch was eyeing the girl with frank admiration. "Well, now, if you was to insist real hard. . . ."

"That's something can be decided later," Sam said, too quickly.

78

Leora apparently didn't sense the crackling hostility. "I was watching how you handled that rope," she told Mitch. "Can you throw a hoolihan?"

"When I'm lucky. It's all in the wrist," he explained, starting to shake out the coil, but then he hesitated and shot a sly look at his brother. "Be glad to show you, but I reckon this ain't the time."

Sam moved his shoulders. "Oh, go ahead," he said gruffly. "Roundup won't stall in its tracks, I guess, if you was to take a few minutes. . . ."

He watched them move off a little way together. He saw how Leora's head tilted back, revealing the graceful column of her brown throat as she laughed merrily at something the young fellow said. They made, Sam realized, a picture of handsome youth, totally absorbed in one another; and the thought put a hollow pang inside him.

He had never thought of himself as an old man. There was actually no great gap in years between himself and Leora, and yet he had to recognize that she was closer to his brother's age than to his own. And a blind man could see that Mitch Cochran, with his youth and charm, had something to which Leora responded with a naive girl's innocent directness.

Sam frowned, not liking to have her so openly attracted to someone as unreliable as Mitch. Or, was that merely a rationalization? Damn it! To be truthful, what he felt just then was a lot closer to the ugly stab of brute jealousy. . . .

Roundup continued on schedule, everything going well; even the weather, after a few days of drizzling cold, cleared and became pleasant enough. The crews of the Northern Division swept like a broom, covering all the miles and swinging steadily nearer to the dividing line at Colter Creek. The occasional word from the south, meanwhile, indicated Morgan Osgood wasn't meeting with any serious delays, either.

Despite Uncle Rupe's angry warning, there'd been no further effort to keep the roundup from working Denker range. Sam Cochran took that on personally, doing a thorough job with his T Square riders and not finding any more evidence of shady practices. Rupe Denker stayed out of his way, scrupulously not interfering. Floyd would no doubt still be laid up with that bullet in the arm, but he was too tough to be put out of action very long. Nor was he or his uncle, either one, apt to swallow a defeat like the one that miserable, damp day at the brush fence. Sometime, somehow, the grudge was certain to be paid off. But Sam couldn't develop a case of nerves, waiting around for it to happen.

It was, instead, another smoldering source of trouble—his differences with Irv Paley—that was the first to flare up in a wholly unexpected moment, with Mitch Cochran the unintending cause. The wagons had moved onto Paley's Hat on a clear warm day when an early buzzing of new-hatched insects gave the afternoon something of the sound and feel of premature midsummer. Here it was that Mitch, combing out a neglected and brush-choked coulee, suddenly jumped a two-year-old and sent him ringing his tail, bounding into the open. He was a real maverick, who had never known hot iron or castrating knife; he had somehow been passed over in previous gathers, probably not once but twice, and he had gone wild.

But Mitch could be as stubborn, when he wanted to be, as anything on four legs. After a session of dodging and cutting back and forth through whipping brush he finally had that renegade brute discouraged. Turning him into the open, he brought him at last to the collection point, and there the two-year maverick became at once a center of interest and lively speculation. Where on earth could an animal that size have been hiding out, and how had he managed to elude not only the previous roundups, but the normal activities of Paley's range crew?

Sam Cochran rode up, listened to some of the speculation, and then called for an end to it with a reminder that this outfit had work to do. He told Mitch to take his find and throw it into the maverick pool—and this was the moment that always-scowling Irv Paley chose for his showdown with the man who had beaten him out of the post of roundup boss.

"The hell you'll throw him with the mavericks," Irv Paley said belligerently. "He's my animal, and I'll put my brand on him."

Sam looked at the man, studying the truculent face with its smashed cheekbone and tangled brows, and guessed that

80

this was one difference of opinion that wouldn't be easily settled. He took his time answering. "Irv," he said finally, "you always been a stickler for custom. You know, as well as anyone here, what's the regular practice with mavericks."

"He's no maverick," Paley retorted. "Maybe once—but he's been eating my grass, for a couple seasons at least; I claim that makes him mine."

"If he carries no brand, he's a maverick," Sam said doggedly. "But I want to be fair. I'm willing to leave it to a vote of the other owners."

He looked around at the suddenly silent group of men. Only Willis Harper and Jim Bowers, among the ranchers, happened to be present. Without hesitation they both shook their heads and Jim Bowers said gruffly, "We can't start making exceptions. Paley knows the rules; let him be governed by them. He's no better than the rest of us."

Irv Paley's face had darkened and a nerve was jumping in one broad cheek. He looked from Bowers to Sam Cochran, and he spoke a word—a foul and angry expletive. "Nobody's taking any vote!" he said harshly. "You done that once before, and I ain't forgetting how it come out! You want this animal? All right then, damn you—take him!" Before anyone could guess what he meant to do, a sixshooter slid into his hand and barked, once. The disputed animal, standing head-lowered and suspicious amid this ring of men and horses, made a sound like a sigh, collapsed as his front legs folded under him, and toppled to the ground.

To the crack of the gun, horses sidestepped nervously. The smoke of the shot hung for a moment in the fly-buzzing stillness, as men stared at the slaughtered animal in stunned surprise. Still defiant, Irv Paley slid the gun back into its holster and deliberately hauled his mount's head smartly about, to a tinkle of bitchains.

Sam Cochran stirred himself, at that, and a long breath swelled his chest. "Paley!"

The man didn't even look around; he had his horse turned, showing Sam his back. This time the latter knew something had to be settled, once and for all, or his authority in the job that he had never wanted would be gone for good. But it was something more—it was a clean, hard anger, at the arrogance of the man and the wanton waste of

81

good beef—that drove his spurs and sent his own horse leaping after the other man.

He had a tendency to be slowmoving, but for once he was so quick that bystanders had to scramble out of his way, and horses were pulled hastily aside to keep from getting rammed. Dirt and grass spurted under the bite of shoe irons as the black lunged after Paley. A couple of bounds and Sam was sawing on the bit, whipping his horse around broadside in front of the Hat rancher and forcing the latter to an uneasy stand.

Sam's voice shook. "By God, I've tried to get along with you! I've swallowed my pride and I've taken more bad manners than anyone has a call to. But this time, you've gone too far! I can't help what you think of me," he went on, trying to keep his anger from making what he said incoherent, "or of my getting the job you wanted so damned much. Fact remains, Paley, it *is* my job."

Irv Paley looked as though he hadn't expected a challenge; he had his hands full at the moment, keeping the nervous horse steady, but he found the arrogance to retort, "You're riding it with a damned high saddle, too!"

"Such ain't my intention," Sam replied, doggedly. "I never asked for it, and I'll give it over in a minute to anyone the roundup chooses. But in the meantime I can't let some spoilsport disrupt everything, by refusing to go along and abide by the rules that govern everybody else.

"As I see it, you owe this roundup a maverick, and you also owe every man here an apology. If nothing but a fight will satisfy you—then, all right: Get out of that saddle and I'll try to give you one. But hurry it up, because the rest of us want to get back to work!"

He had never seen anything quite like the expression on Irv Paley's face. It looked mottled, behind its bristling brows and heavy mustache. A shadow flickered at the corner of the man's jaw, where a muscle seemed to be caught in a kind of spasm. But then all expression smoothed out and his thick chest lifted on an indrawn breath. "The hell with it!" he exclaimed, in an oddly muffled voice, and in the next moment he pulled wide of Sam Cochran and rode off toward his own wagon, spurring hard.

Sam was left staring after the Hat rancher. He turned as Jim Bowers, a stooped and baldheaded caricature of a man on his big roan horse, eased over to join him. Bowers wore a look of sour approval. "Good for you!" he grunted. "You made him back down. Damned if I don't think you scared him out!"

"I dunno about that." Sam shook his head, puzzled and troubled. "I shouldn't have lost my temper. I never meant to scare him and I doubt that I did. He's tough, and he knows it."

Bowers lifted a bony shoulder. "Well—whatever. If only he talks a mite quieter around here, we got reason enough to thank you. Because, backing away like that, he's sure as hell going to have mighty little room left to talk!" He turned away, then, to indicate the slaughtered beef and tell a couple of the punchers, "Somebody get rid of that damn thing. The cooks can use the meat. . . ."

Sam Cochran felt the letdown, after the anger and tension of a scene that, after all, as far as he could tell, seemed to have come to nothing. He pulled off his hat, ran a wrist across his forehead. Afterward, picking up the reins again, he happened to catch his brother staring at him.

He had forgotten Mitch, but the young fellow had been there, of course, for that whole encounter. And, meeting his look, Sam discovered something in it he hadn't seen before. For a fact, the boy appeared to be impressed. In that moment his rebellious dislike seemed to be tempered grudgingly with something almost like respect.

But if it was true he turned away to his horse without saying anything. Sam was left frowning and unhappy over the whole miserable occurrence.

CHAPTER XII

Only a handful had witnessed the showdown between Sam Cochran and Irv Paley, but those who did wasted no time in spreading the story. It ran through the camp, passed from mouth to mouth at cookfires or wherever two or more of the roundup crew got together for a few words of idle talk. And like all such talk, it grew and became unreliable.

Leora Tabbart heard the rumors, the very next day when she rode out from T Square headquarters. She didn't quite trust them, but nevertheless they bothered her; a frank and forthright person, she would have gone straight to Sam for clarification except that he was off somewhere that day, and she didn't get a chance. Instead she went to Mitch Cochran, who after all had been present and should have known exactly what went on.

She got her chance to raise the subject as the two of them, with Vic Bonner, were pushing a jag of beef toward T Square range through a golden haze of late afternoon. Letting the beasts set their own pace, she and Mitch talked as they rode stirrup to stirrup:

"But just what did Irv Paley *say*?"

"Didn't say much of anything," the young fellow answered. "Not after Sam had got through giving him a lacing down. Far as I could see, he just took it."

The girl shook her head. "I only hope he doesn't try to get even, some way. He's always struck me as the kind who can be mean, and he's held a grudge ever since this roundup got under way. Even though it wasn't poor Sam's fault at all!"

" 'Poor Sam!' " Mitch repeated, with a hint of sarcasm. "No need your feeling sorry for *him*. He's got a hide like an ox."

"Oh, you're wrong! He's a very sensitive person."

Mitch gave her a look, as though wondering if they could

84

be discussing the same man. But he let it go with a shrug. "Well, if Paley had no cause to be sore, it's more'n made up for now. Sam really roughed him with his tongue. Paley looked pretty black when he rode away from it."

"Oh, dear!" Leora exclaimed. "That's just what has me worried. . . ."

There was an end to talk, for a while, as the cattle they were trailing fed down through a break and onto a well-watered, grassy piece of flat where they were to be held. Jane Tabbart had an order from a feed-lot outfit that wanted eight hundred head of good stock for immediate range delivery. The price offered was a good one and, since T Square was overstocked for the amount of its summer grass, on Sam Cochran's advice Jane had taken the deal. The shipping herd was being built on this stretch of pasture where there was grass and water to hold them; they were in a natural pocket and wouldn't stray.

Joining the two men at the edge of the meadow, Leora looked at the sun that hung low above the ragged western rim. "Time for me to be going in. Mama's been baking, today—there'll be fresh bread, and enough pie that all the boys at our wagon can at least have a sliver. Either or both of you care to come along with me and tote it back to camp?"

She'd made the invitation inclusive; but Vic Bonner, looking from the girl to Mitch Cochran and back again, made his guess and a quick decision. The deep-set eyes in the wrinkled face nearly lost themselves in his sly grin, as he said, "Sounds like a job for a younger man than me. I'll leave it to the kid."

"Why, sure," Mitch agreed instantly. "Put the bread in a sack, and I'll hang it from my saddlehorn. And I'll manage the pies, if I have to hold them on my lap the whole distance."

From Leora's expression it should have been evident to anyone this was how she had hoped it would work out. Bonner, taking up the reins, told her in mock seriousness, "Be sure you count them pies, so he can't eat 'em all before he gets there!" He lifted his horse with the spurs then, soon losing himself in the sage and scattered timber. And the two young people turned and, side by side, began the ride to T Square.

Today was the first chance Leora had really had for a talk with Mitch, and there was a great deal about this young man and his background she wanted to know. "What was it like at home?" she urged him. "When you were boys together? Sam's never told me a word."

"Likely enough," he said, "because there ain't nothing worth telling. Pa was a dull sort—like Sam, thataway. There was a passel of us kids and no more than enough to go around. So, Sam took off early; and I did too, soon as I could shake loose."

"Were you trying to follow Sam?"

"Why would I do that? Only lead me to some place as dull as what we left! No, there's a lot of places to this world and I wanted to see me a few. And I done it, some."

"I've never been out of Colter Basin," the girl said wistfully. "Except when Papa took me to Denver with him once, only I was too little to remember."

"Well, I feel sorry for you. Couldn't begin to name all the places I seen, these last few years. Why, I been clear to Frisco."

"No!"

"Fact! And K.C., and north as far as Missoula, south nearly to Mexico. . . ." Finding her a rapt and eager audience, he proceeded to expand on this bare itinerary; and if all the things he spun out, as they drifted on toward T Square through the gold of fading day, were, perhaps, not hewn strictly to the line of sober truth—still, Leora was a naive and trusting girl and failed to know the difference.

Within a quarter mile of ranch headquarters, now, they had halted their mounts by unspoken agreement while she listened, breathlessly, to Mitch's yarn about a man in Wichita who had tried to cheat him out of a month's wages, and how he had dealt with the situation. Eyes wide, she shook her head a little as he finished. "It's strange," she murmured. "For brothers, you and Sam are so completely different!"

"That's plenty true enough," he said, as though pleased to agree with her. "He handled Irv Paley and the Denkers but most of the time he's a sure-enough stick in the mud!" There was a new, speculative look to the young fellow's eyes, suddenly; he had moved his horse in closer to the girl, who appeared not to notice that his knee was now pressed

86

against hers. His voice had dropped a few tones, taken on a new quality. He said, "Why, to think of the opportunities he's had, and how little he's done with them—it's enough to make you sick!"

The girl's blue eyes, so close to his own, frowned at him in puzzlement. "What opportunities? I don't know what you mean. He's foreman; and he works hard. . . ."

"I ain't talkin' about range chores," Mitch said roughly. "What I see is a damn fool who don't know even the first thing about dealing with a woman, like she wants to be dealt with. Here he is, spending hours every day with as eye-filling a piece as I ever seen in a skirt—and he don't even appreciate it! He talks cows and tick dip, when he ought to know a little girl like you is waitin' to hear something else entirely."

Leora stiffened. She knew little of men but suddenly she could tell she was involved with something she hadn't bargained for. She started a protest, as Mitch Cochran's arm slipped smoothly about her shoulders. His other hand groped for her waist; leaning from the saddle, he drew her to him and his mouth came down hard upon her own.

For just a moment her astonishment was such that she lay motionless in his grasp, unable to think or move. Then shocked indignation burst in full flower; she gave a squeal of protest that was trapped against the unyielding pressure of his lips. She tried to turn her head away but was unable. Her hands came against his chest and she struggled to push free, but it was the movement of the horses, stirring under them and threatening to unseat them both, that forced Mitch Cochran to release her.

They broke apart. Mitch caught his balance and grinned as he looked at the girl, who had lost her flat-crowned hat in the struggle. It hung from its throatlatch, freeing her brown hair in a tangle; her face was white with anger and she had the back of a hand pressed against her lips.

Her voice trembled. "Why, how could you?" she gasped. "Don't you ever try that again!"

Mitch only grinned, totally unabashed. "Who you kidding? You know you enjoyed it!"

But she was already pulling the reins, to back away and give her horse maneuvering space, and now without another word she swung her bridles and kicked the little mare into a run, toward the house. As she went she heard Mitch Cochran's laugh behind her; her face was aflame with shame and hurt.

She was nearly there before she realized Mitch was coming right after her. The claybank plowed to a dust-lifting halt; as she leaped from saddle the man's hand descended on her shoulder. "Hey! You act like you're really mad!" he exclaimed, that humiliating note of amusement in his voice. "I never hurt you none!" Leora ducked from under his fingers and, whirling, backed away; her breast lifted to the swell of anger inside her.

"Don't you touch me!" she cried, furious with herself as she felt the hot sting of uncontrollable tears.

"Look! I didn't mean—"

His mocking stare shifted from her; his words broke off and his face slowly lost all expression. At the same moment Leora heard the slap of the screen door going closed, and she twisted about. Her mother stood on the porch, glaring at the young man in the claybank's saddle. The level rays of the low sun struck full upon Jane Tabbart's angry, tight-lipped face, and it made the twin barrels of the shotgun in her hands shine with a glint almost of burnished brass.

Jane said grimly, "You have until I count five!"

Mitch looked into the double eye of the shotgun and his face lost shape and color. His mouth opened and closed again. Leora saw the look in her mother's eye and terror struck through her and left her knees weak. "No, Mama!" she managed to exclaim. "No—it's all right!"

The older woman showed no sign of relenting. The ugly looking weapon remained rockhard and steady in her work-roughened hands as she said, with harsh firmness, "It's a long way from all right! When some saddletramp thinks all he has to do is ride into a place where two women are alone, and—"

"He's not a saddletramp, Mama. He's—" She caught herself. "He works for us."

That had enough effect to put uncertainty into the older woman's frown, but the shotgun never wavered. She looked at her daughter as she repeated, "For us? I don't know him."

"I'm right new here, ma'am," Mitch put in quickly. His

fear of the weapon seemed already dissipated; his white teeth flashed in his most engaging smile, and he was nodding in relaxed and friendly fashion as he reached to pull off his hat. "Mitch Cochran's the name."

"Cochran. . . ." Jane Tabbart stared at him, and then looked to Leora for explanation. With a tremulous sigh the girl nodded.

"Mama, he's Sam's brother. He's been helping out on roundup. He's a very good hand. . . ."

Now, at last, Jane let the shotgun swing down until its muzzles pointed at the boards beneath her feet; but she was still far from satisfied. She ran her smoldering look from Leora, standing by her horse and trying now to paw some order into the tangle of her hair and set her hat in place, back to the strange young man in the claybank's saddle. She said sternly, "So—you're trading on your brother's position here at T Square! Well, just don't think you can carry it too far. Because, if I see again anything remotely like what I just now did, you will be drawing your time and clearing off this ranch within five minutes flat. Is that perfectly clear?"

"Why, sure, Miz Tabbart." The cocky grin didn't waver in its brashness. "Leora knows I was only teasing. We're good friends."

"You're not *that* good a friend," Jane snapped back at him, "and don't you forget it! Now—turn that horse and head back to roundup camp, and after this try to behave yourself."

"Whatever you say, ma'am." To the girl he added, "What about the grub I was to take back with me?"

Leora explained her purpose in bringing Mitch to headquarters. The older woman listened coldly, gave Mitch another disapproving look. She said curtly, "I'll fetch it. He can stay where he's at." She turned again to the screen door. As it slapped shut, Leora looked again uneasily at the young fellow on the claybank.

She said earnestly, "Mitch, I never meant to get you in trouble. But, honestly—"

"No apologies necessary," he said genially.

"I wasn't apologizing!" she retorted; his easy and unabashed acceptance of what had happened raised a new spark of anger. "Really! I don't know what kind of girls

89

you're acquainted with; but after this I hope you'll save that sort of thing for—for some of the others!" She felt her cheeks grow warm, even as she said it.

Mitch grinned knowingly, but what he might have answered was lost as Jane Tabbart appeared again, darkly, beyond the screen door. She didn't seem to like to see the two of them together, for she said sharply, "Leora! I want you to come and help me."

"Yes, Mama." A final, searching look for the man in the saddle, and she turned and hurried up the steps into the house. Mitch sat and watched her go, while the first breath of evening plucked at his horse's mane and made the lingering sunlight dance in the tall cottonwood heads behind the house.

CHAPTER XIII

The Sunday that had come and passed, now, had been for Colter Basin merely another work-filled day, in an unbroken stretch of them. The crews had stayed in the field, with no break in their labors which had settled into a routine and a rhythm that could not be allowed to lose momentum. The town and the home ranches lay silent, in a half-life of waiting which had come to seem almost a normal thing.

Roundup had entered its second week. The men who came in from the field, at rare intervals, were not the same as when they had ridden out a few short days ago. They had begun to wear the look of battle veterans—cheeks starting to stretch taut behind masks of grime and beardstubble, as immediate reserves of strength and muscle were spent and the rest of the job had to be toughed out on nerve and endurance alone. They spoke little. They completed whatever errand had brought them in and returned to their saddles, and with an odd mingling of reluctance and impatience rode off again, and the dust and empty, sunfilled distances swallowed them up.

Below Colter Creek, the Southern Division had swung into the concluding phase of its operations. This brought it onto Morgan Osgood's grass; and Sybil Osgood, returning to Clawhammer headquarters in early afternoon from another meeting in the hills with John Harnett, narrowly missed running into some of her husband's men moving cattle.

She heard the bawling of the steers and saw the dust, barely in time to rein out of the way. Moments later she pulled up in a fringe of pines and held the strawberry roan there as, with pulses racing, she peered through the branches to watch a tide of red hides and flashing horns funnel down through a draw. Across the heated stillness she could hear, distinctly, the rumble of hoofs and the thin shouts of the riders pushing the animals ahead of them. The dust rose and the horsemen drifted through it, whirling ropes and slashing at the flanks of the cattle to keep them moving.

It had been a bad fright, and Sybil took a moment to regain control. Actually, had she been seen she supposed she could have invented an excuse to explain her presence here, away from the ranch—she had done it before. But it was humiliating that she couldn't consider herself free to come and go however she pleased.

She was the mistress of Clawhammer, wasn't she? Or—was she, rather, its prisoner?

She had once felt supremely sure of herself here, with a confidence that had helped to compensate for the numbing years of genteel poverty before her marriage to Morgan Osgood had saved her from all that. Now, however, some of John Harnett's fear about their clandestine meetings was beginning at last to rub off on her. Once she had felt a certain awe of the wealth and power Morgan Osgood very obviously represented; later, when it was too late and she had seen him as a part of this dreary, hated part of the world to which she had committed herself, the awe had given way to a kind of contempt.

Today this was all changed. Today she was literally afraid of him. . . . .

When she decided the chances of discovery were past, she turned the roan out of that clot of trees and put him on a different route, swinging wide of the place where she had watched cattle and riders disappear. But she rode now with a panicky alertness, for she had seen there was no way of knowing from what quarter men of the roundup might unexpectedly appear—they could be all around her.

Once, in fact, she caught sight of the Division camp, some distance away across an open expanse of bunch grass and sagebrush. She saw the wagons and the smoke of the cookfires, the loose-bunched horses, the dust that hung in a canopy above the mill of the collection herd. She saw the figures of men working around the area, and even the drab shape of the canvas tent Morgan Osgood always pitched for his personal headquarters. Sybil rode wide of this place and only breathed easily again when she had left it well behind her. After that she used her braided quirt and sent the roan at a good clip, straight toward the ranch. She would not feel safe until she reached it.

Bitter disillusionment with the world she had married into had come to her on the day she first set foot in the yard at Clawhammer. The shapeless, sprawling main house was, to her, haphazard and boundlessly ugly, and the heavy graceless furnishings even more so. Everything inside was permeated, hopelessly, by the stink of the cigars that Osgood never left off smoking. And there were those other, far worse smells—Osgood seemed neither to notice nor to care that he had built his barns and horse corrals much too carelessly near his living quarters. Nor would he likely consider moving them.

Not a flower, a tree, nor even a blade of grass grew anywhere in the hard-packed dirt of the ranch yard, but in front of the veranda was set a long, unsightly, tooth-marked hitch pole—her home might as well have been a saloon, or perhaps something even worse, on the main street in town.

Her one thought, as she cantered her lathered roan into this masculine place that she loathed and hated, was to get the horse into the corral, the saddle off and hanging in its place, the sweated blanket spread and drying. In order to reach the corral she must pass the front of the house. She turned the corner and suddenly her hand was tightening on the rein as she caught sight of the big, rawboned gray— Morgan Osgood's favorite riding horse—standing under saddle at the tiepole. Raising her eyes to the deep veranda, then, she saw her husband.

Osgood sat in a low, leather-slung chair, his hat pushed to the back of his head, a stub of a cigar clamped between his jaws, a glass half-filled with whisky in his rope-scarred fist. The bottle sat on the boards beside him. His legs were crossed, the sole of one heavy boot showing a glob of cow manure stuck to it beneath the instep. The breath stopped in her throat as she saw he was watching her from beneath lowered brows, with a wordless intensity.

There was no evading the issue. Sybil forced herself to ride ahead under the weight of his stare, put her horse to the pole beside his own and stepped down there. She took longer than she needed fastening a knot in the reins, as she worked to collect her thoughts. Afterward, filling her lungs, she moved to the broad steps and mounted them. She placed a hand against a roof support pillar and forced herself to meet her husband's cold stare.

"Nice ride?" Morg Osgood asked, a hint of sarcasm veiling the words.

She shrugged. "It was all right."

Osgood plucked the cigar from his lips, raised his glass and drained off what was left of his drink. Sybil tried to take advantage of this moment to move across the porch to the door, without too obvious haste. Her hand was almost on the latch when her husband stopped her with another question. "Where did you go?"

"Why, nowhere actually." She made her answer as casual and indifferent as she was able. "You know—I just wanted to get away for a little, get some fresh air."

She could not see his face. Waiting, she watched the heavy shoulder and the back of his head as Osgood leaned to set his empty glass on the floor. He said gruffly, "I been setting here the best part of an hour—time I didn't have to spare. Here I come in for a moment with my wife, and she ain't even home. . . ."

"I'm sorry." Her hand reached again for the latch. "I really must change out of these things."

"You go do that," he agreed. He added, before she could move, "But first ain't you got so much as a kiss for your husband who's been setting here waiting all this time?"

He cocked a look at her, then, and to Sybil it seemed a leering mockery. She steeled herself not to show the revulsion she felt, as she turned reluctantly across the porch to him. When she bent above him, the odors of whisky and cigar smoke and sweated clothing were almost more than she could bear.

And then the expression of her husband's heavy face changed, subtly; a hand closed upon her wrist. He almost snarled; "Suppose you tell me—where do you meet him?"

She thought she would faint. "I—don't know what you mean!"

"I've had a bellyful of lying!" Morg Osgood retorted. A twist at her wrist brought her suddenly to her knees beside him, made her fingers open and drop the leather quirt. Sybil barely bit back a cry of pain as the chair arm struck hard against one full breast.

With a savage gesture, Osgood flung the much-chewed butt of the cigar in an arc, over the railing to hard-packed ground below. His fingers bore down relentlessly upon her wrist. "I know what's been going on," he told her harshly.

"So—the fewer lies, the better it'll go for you!" His eyes bored into hers, his mouth grew ugly. "My God! To be played for a fool—and for a man like that!"

Somewhere she found the courage to answer the contempt in his voice and in his eyes. "That's something you wouldn't understand! He, at least, is a gentleman!"

"*Him?*" A roar, partly laughter and partly a sound of pure rage, broke from the man's thick chest. "A gentleman? Sam Cochran?"

Sybil was left staring at the blocky face so near her own—forgetful, at that moment, of the pain of her trapped wrist and the agony in her breast. Sam Cochran! It rushed in upon her, then—what John had told her, about the mistake Grif Storrs had made and passed on to his employer. Suddenly she felt that she was going to give way to a fit of hysterical laughter; she felt it welling inside her, managed instead to smother it in a cry: "You're breaking my arm. . . ."

"Like hell!" the man grunted, but he released her with a savage thrust that nearly flung her sprawling. "It's an idea that tempts me," he said, "so you'd best be careful. Now—get out of my sight!" And he swung to his feet, shoving back his chair, and the boards of the porch creaked beneath heavy cowhide boots as he moved around her and down the steps into the yard.

Sybil Osgood pulled herself to her feet, and fled into the house.

In her room, with the door shut, she fumbled to turn the key in the lock and then leaned her shoulders against the panel, while the aftermath of that scene shook her and turned her knees to water. Her first coherent thought was that, somehow, she must warn John Harnett. There was this brief reprieve, but it could not serve for very long. For the moment her husband had been put off the track, turned instead against Sam Cochran. But, once confronted with the charge, the fellow couldn't be expected to let the error stand for long. He would tell what he knew of her and the doctor, and he could hardly fail to convince Morgan Osgood that it was the truth.

The bedroom window was open, and now Sybil became aware of a murmur of voices in the yard. She stepped to look down, keeping back from sight within the hang of the window curtains. Down there, in the full sunlight and

95

foreshortened beneath the wide brims of their hats, her husband stood talking with two of his men. It was impossible to catch what was being said, but once she heard Grif Storrs's name spoken, on a rising inflection. One of the men nodded, said something, and then turned to mount the horse that he held by its reins. He rode out of the yard, evidently on a mission to locate Grif Storrs with a message from his chief.

That taken care of, Morgan Osgood turned to give some instruction to his second man, and afterward heeled about and strode out of her line of sight, in the direction of the veranda. A minute later he reappeared, mounted on his gray, and rode out of the yard on a line that evidently pointed toward his roundup headquarters. Sybil watched him from sight, then cut her glance again to that lone figure left standing in the yard below her window. He, in his turn, having watched his chief's departure, swung about and walked slowly toward the house, like a man who had his orders.

Sybil Osgood, with bitterness and alarm, could guess what those orders must be. From this moment, she knew she was being watched. The intent, of course, was to keep her from taking warning to Sam Cochran; but as a result her hands were tied. Sick with despair, she saw there was no way now she could let John Harnett know of the danger that, sooner or later, would be closing in on him.

There was nothing she could do, at all.

Shortly after they crossed north over Colter Creek, Grif Storrs and his two companions came across a pair of Willis Harper's riders watering their horses at a tributary spring. Grif asked them without preliminary, "Know where we'd find Sam Cochran?"

"Why, he's just about all over the place," one answered, while his stare took in the trio from across the creek.

The two men Storrs had brought with him were Clawhammer men—Reuben Choate, a big fellow with a mean scowl, and Neil Wiley whose strangely sunken eyes were almost lost beneath a shelf of black brow. All three were armed, and they had a keen intentness about them that made the second Harper crewman suggest quickly, "You best try the camp. It's on the flats east of Ryan's Creek, just below them potholes. Quickest way to get there—"

"I know how to get there," Storrs interrupted, and gave his reins a jerk that sawed the bit and made his animal toss its head. The three of them rode off without another word, lifting into a lope, and left the punchers staring after them.

"What do you suppose is chewing *him*?" the first one demanded. "Trouble at the other Division, maybe?"

The second puncher slowly shook his head. "Somehow I got the feeling it was trouble for Sam Cochran. . . ."

Ryan's Creek flowed swift and deep among the potholes it had scoured out, then shallowed and gentled as it hit the flats below. This was the southwestern edge of Tabbart grass, and a good place to set up a holding point. Grif Storrs and his companions had the T Square wagon pointed out to them and, skirting the activity at the beef herd, rode over there; hands piled on saddlehorn, the Clawhammer foreman put his question to Smitty whose arms were white with flour, clear to the rolled-up shirtsleeves.

Smitty shook his head. "Naw, Sam rode out alone this morning and he ain't back. Wanted to check that range up toward the head of the creek, and then he was gonna swing by the Buttes, see if it looked like he'd need to send a crew in there tomorrow."

"Alone, you said?" Storrs echoed. "Been gone all day?" Storrs turned and shared a slow, significant exchange of looks with Choate and Wiley; his thin lips quirked, in what could have been a knowing smile of triumph.

Reuben Choate rubbed a wrist across his heavy jaw. "What do we do?"

"Why, looks as if we wait a while. By my figuring, our boy should be riding in just any time now." Storrs looked back at the cook, indicated the big graniteware pot with a jerk of his blond head. "Any coffee there?"

"Sure. . . ." Smitty wiped the flour from his hands onto his apron, and fetched tin cups. The three from the Southern Division dismounted by the wagon, taking their time, and dropped reins to anchor their horses. Storrs poured the coffee and passed the cups around.

Smitty said, "I hope you ain't got bad news for Sam."

Storrs lifted one thick shoulder. "You might call it a message for him. From Osgood. . . ."

They took their time with the coffee and had very little to say; but word of their presence and their unexplained mission spread quickly through the camp. It reached the ears of Jane Tabbart, who was paying one of her infrequent visits to the roundup camp now that it was situated so near to T Square's home ranch. She came toward the fire, tooling a buckboard and team over the thick wire grass and hummocky meadow soil of the flat. She wore her poke bonnet to protect her from the sun and she handled the reins expertly. She halted her rig beside the fire. "Mister Storrs," she said.

The man nodded briefly, half-raising a finger to hatbrim. The black eyes in the strange, wedge-shaped face held their secrets. "Ma'am. . . ."

"I understand you're asking for my foreman. Is there anything I can help you with?"

Storrs seemed to consider, though the secretive hint of a smile never left his mouth. "Why, no," he said with elaborate casualness. "This is sort of a private matter."

And Neil Wiley echoed his tone: "Personal, you might say."

On the buckboard's seat Jane Tabbart looked from one to the other, puzzled and beginning to feel both anger and alarm at the way her every tentative suggestion bounced off the closed surface they presented. "Well," she said lamely, frowning, "I just thought—"

And then she broke off, as a sudden word from Reuben Choate called the foreman's attention to the single rider approaching. It was Cochran, sure enough. Even as they watched they saw Art James ride up and intercept him, say something that made Sam lift his head and look long in the direction of the fire. He made some answer and with a nod to the puncher, he came on. And Grif Storrs very deliberately finished off his coffee and spilled the dregs into the fire, and there was a brief clatter as all three Clawhammer men tossed their empty cups into the wreck pan.

They turned then, spreading out just a shade, and Storrs stepped forward as Sam Cochran pulled his black horse to a stand. Sam looked at Jane Tabbart, on the buckboard's seat, and then at the men from Clawhammer. He said, "You want me, Grif?"

"Damn right," the Osgood foreman answered heavily. "And don't bother to get off your saddle. We're takin' you with us. . . ."

CHAPTER XIV

Sam Cochran straightened a little in the saddle, a frown shaping his blunt features. "I don't think I'm going anywhere with you, Grif," he said shortly. "Just the same, maybe you better give me some idea what this is all about!"

"You sure you want that? In front of everybody?" Storrs glanced around as he said it. From everywhere, it seemed, curious men were beginning to drift toward the T Square wagon like filings to a magnet. A circle was taking form, Sam and the Clawhammer riders and Jane Tabbart's buckboard at the center. Grif Storrs shrugged. "It's nothing to me, if you don't mind having it known that you and Osgood's woman have been playing around!"

Sam understood, then. "I see." A stir of reaction in the group about them sharpened his tone. "You're making a mistake, Grif."

"*You* made the mistake!" Storrs retorted. "And you ain't going to get off, this time, with anything as light as a little beating up. Not if I judge the mood the old man is in!"

Jane Tabbart spoke, her eyes on her foreman. "Just what is he saying, Sam? Is there any truth at all in this?"

Sam shook his head. "No." But his heart sank a little at what he read in her expression.

"Oh, he'll deny it, of course," Storrs said, a sneer on his wedge-shaped face. "But we know what we know—don't we, Sam? Now, me, I'm not even sore at you, not the way Morgan is. Hell, I could even be a little bit grateful. Now that you've shown him the kind of tramp he took in, maybe he'll get rid of her and Clawhammer can go back to being the outfit it used to."

Drawing a breath, Sam demanded, "Does Mrs. Osgood claim I was mixed up with her?"

"She ain't saying nothing, according to Morg. But she ain't denying it, either."

No, Sam thought—she wouldn't. As long as her husband's suspicions were directed toward the wrong man, she would welcome the chance to protect John Harnett. And Harnett, for his part, was not the stuff that heroes were made of. He wouldn't come forward and take his blame—especially not when chance, and Sam's own bungling effort to keep his brother out of trouble, had provided him with a scapegoat.

For the moment there was nothing to say. Sam could feel the weight of all these eyes on him, and the dark suspicion that made of Jane Tabbart's face something he didn't very much like to look at. Now Grif Storrs, getting no more argument, turned to the pair who had ridden here with him. "Mount up, and we'll be going. . . ."

Sam wanted them in their saddles, so he held his tongue while Storrs and Wiley and Choate found their stirrups. But as they settled into the leather, he quietly drew his gun and eased the hammer back. He reached over, laying his wrist on his left thigh to steady the aim. He said, "You'll go without me, Grif."

That caused a stir. The foreman's blond head whipped around; he saw the gun pointed at him and his face flooded with color, while his hand transmitted an involuntary jerk to the reins and made the horse sidestep under him. But though he had a sixshooter in his own belt holster, and a carbine under his knee, he was careful to do nothing that could be interpreted as a move toward either one.

He spoke in a voice gone suddenly hoarse: "Cochran, you're going to regret this!"

"I'd regret it more," Sam said, "if I went along meekly like you want me to. I did that once, and I took another man's punishment; it won't happen again. You go and tell Osgood that. I ain't running away—I'll be here, if he wants to see me and straighten this out. But, he's been misinformed."

Grif Storrs's oath mingled with a sudden cry of warning—Sam never knew who spoke it. Nor did he ever really know if Reuben Choate, partly blocked as he was by the figure of Storrs, actually tried for a gun or not. But there was some convulsive movement, there, and Sam's reflexes leaped in an effort to swing his own sixshooter over.

The move was startled, wholly unintended, and in making it his wrist struck the saddlehorn, hard. His finger jarred the trigger and the explosion flipped the weapon from his grasp. Empty handed, he sat while the black curvetted nervously under him, and stared at Grif Storrs.

The man was crumpling, doubling forward. He had lost his hat as the strike of the bullet caused his head to whiplash. Lank yellow hair fell into black eyes and a face gone slackly expressionless. And then Neil Wiley was trying to hold his boss in the saddle, but Grif Storrs slid right out of his hands and dropped limply into the dirt.

In the stunned stillness that followed that single pistol shot, Sam Cochran heard a voice say foolishly, "No—no!" and recognized it for his own. He swung down, but could only stand rooted and useless; for Reuben Choate had already dismounted and was on one knee beside the hurt man, and plainly there was nothing he or anyone else could do. Storrs lay on his back, arms and legs thrown wide; the whole front of his shirt began to turn a brilliant red. His chest rose and fell in a fluttering, shallow breathing that was painful to watch.

His back arched, stiffened; the blood gushed from between his jaws, and then he collapsed and the breathing and the outpouring of blood were stilled. It took him no longer than that to die.

Reuben Choate was the first to stir himself. He came to his feet, standing over Storrs's lifeless body, and a stare of pure hatred sought Cochran's face and settled there. "By God, it was murder! You all seen it!"

Sam tried to speak but all the moisture was dried out of his mouth and his jaws seemed to cleave together. "Grif never even touched a gun," Choate went on doggedly. "But this bastard shot him anyway. And I call it murder!"

Vic Bonner objected, in a voice that was hoarse with shock. "Choate, it was an accident! Sam never meant to fire."

"That's the truth," Sam said, finding his tongue. "I couldn't help it. I knocked my hand against the horn. . . ."

Choate's expression was changeless, completely uncon-

vinced. "Ain't how *I* seen it!" he retorted. "But, the
important thing is how it's gonna look to Morg Osgood!"
Without warning, a weapon was in his hand and its muzzle
gaped at Sam, across the few yards that separated them.
"You can leave your gun on the ground and get back on that
horse. You'll answer to Morg, for this."

"No, he won't."

Sam Cochran, caught staring at the muzzle of the Colt,
turned in slow astonishment as he heard the interruption.
The new speaker, incredibly enough, was Irv Paley; Sam's
fiercest critic among the North Basin ranchers had shoved
in between a couple of the silently watching roundup crew,
and now the rifle that he held in his two hands—right fist
closed upon the breech action, the other supporting the
gleaming tube—was pointed straight at the buckle of
Reuben Choate's belt.

"You see what I got here, don't you?" Paley warned; and
the tone of his voice and the truculent scowl on his battered
face were equally dangerous. "I guess we all know what
would happen if Osgood was to get his hands on Cochran,
after *this*—so, just forget it. Throw that sixshooter away or
else put it back in the holster. You too, Wiley!" A thrust of
his scowling stare, lifted toward the second Clawhammer
rider who was still in the saddle, included him in the
warning. "Don't you be making any mistakes, either of
you!"

Nothing could have been more astonishing for Sam
Cochran than to have Irv Paley come to his assistance. He
frankly stared, more weighty matters forgotten and his own
tongue stilled; it was Vic Bonner who produced a short gun
from somewhere and echoed Paley's warning: "You better
pay close attention to what Irv is saying. . . ."

"So that's how it is?" Choate's face had taken on angry
color as he looked around him, but he had to respect a pair
of weapons leveled at him. He swung his head like a baited
bull and said heavily, "You needn't think Osgood will settle
for this!"

"The man is right," Sam said, though it cost him an
effort. "This is between me and Osgood, and I don't like
other people getting caught in it. I better go have it out."

Paley shook his head, adamant. "You're a fool if you do.
At least, give Clawhammer time to cool off."

That made sense, and Sam nodded as he recognized it. Reuben Choate, then, must have seen that he wasn't going to have his way. He swore, and thrust the gun back into his holster. "We'll see," he muttered darkly, "what Osgood has to say. Somebody at least give me a hand, here."

A couple of the men stepped forward to help him with Grif Storrs. It was a grisly thing, to watch that limp and starchless figure being handed up and slung across his saddle, arms and legs lolling. There seemed a tremendous lot of blood; it got onto the hands and clothing of the men who lifted him, it smeared the saddle and made the dead man's horse snort and start and show the whites of its eyes, as it caught the scent. Sam felt something rise in his throat and he looked away, swallowing it back.

He couldn't bring himself to look at Jane Tabbart who had all this time been seated in the buckboard, not uttering a sound.

Choate hooked the dead foreman's belt over the saddlehorn to hold it and made a fast tie with Storrs's own saddle rope. He pulled the knots fast with a savage jerk, then got into his own saddle and took the reins of the dead man's horse to lead it. His own mount moving uneasily under him, he looked down at Sam Cochran and had a parting shot: "This ain't the end of it, by any means. Mister, you can believe me, I wouldn't want to be in *your* boots! You got a lot to answer for—and you ain't even begun answering!"

A jerk of his head at Neil Wiley, and he swung his bridles and the group moved back to give plenty of room. The three who had ridden here from Clawhammer rode away again—only, one was now a grotesquely swaying burden, roped across his own saddle. They lifted dust and afterward struck the shallow course of Ryan's Creek, raising a brief curtain of hoof-chopped stream water as they splashed to the opposite bank. And then they were gone.

Sam Cochran saw his gun lying on the ground and he leaned and got it, put it back into the holster without bothering about the shell he'd emptied. He looked around, then, to find that nearly every eye was resting on him, waiting. Where Storrs had fallen, there was a rich red stain of blood on the ground; Vic Bonner was using his boots to scuff dirt over it and bury it.

Sam squared his shoulders. "I hope," he said, "nobody
103

here thinks for a minute I *meant* to kill him! It was pure accident—and that's the Lord's truth!"

From the buckboard's seat, Jane Tabbart spoke. "Does it matter how it happened?"

"I suppose not," he had to agree. "It don't change the facts: Storrs is dead—and Morg Osgood's not going to take it lightly." Sam Cochran hesitated, hating what he knew must be said. He drew a breath. "Under the circumstances maybe it'd be best if I give you my resignation."

Jane looked at him squarely. "Yes," she said. "Maybe it would."

"All right. . . ."

Her quickness to accept hurt, just a little. A heaviness settled in him but Sam tried not to show it as he nodded, woodenly. It was Vic Bonner who voiced a protest. The old puncher stepped over and laid a rope-tough palm on the iron wheel rim, as he looked in astonishment and disbelief at the woman on the seat. "Ma'am!" he exclaimed. "I know it ain't for me to say, but—in Bob Tabbart's day, this brand sure would never have turned against one of its own. Just when he most needed it to back him!"

She turned an angry stare upon the man; before she could answer, Sam put in quickly, "It isn't quite the same, Vic. This has nothing to do with the brand. It's a matter I've got to work out myself." He looked again at Jane. "Don't worry. I'll get my stuff, and pull out. It will be better all around."

"I agree." Her words were clipped, her eyes' without warmth or friendliness.

Vic Bonner persisted: "But we ain't even finished the damned roundup!"

At that, Sam had to smile a little. "I reckon you can manage it without me." A glance at the others standing around, and he added dryly, "Might be an idea if you got this crowd back to it, right now. The show is over; they all got jobs to do. I don't need them to see me off."

They actually began to break up, on that. First a man here and a couple yonder, they split and started drifting away—even though reluctantly, with dragging boots and their heads turned for a final look. A murmur of voices began to rise, as an excited discussion began that was going to take a long time cooling down, across campfires and bunkshack poker games for months to come.

But a good many who were still in earshot heard what happened next. Sam had found the stirrup and swung up and as he settled into the leather Jane Tabbart told him crisply, "You'll do me a favor if you'll take that worthless brother of yours with you, when you go."

Slowly, astonished at the vehemence in her words, Sam turned. He said, frowning, "You're talking about Mitch. But I won't pretend I understand you."

"No." She lifted one shoulder. "I don't suppose he did tell you what happened between him and my daughter, two days ago. And Leora made me promise I wouldn't!"

Something like a black illness at the pit of the stomach began to spread through Sam. "I'll take it kindly, ma'am, if you'll tell me now. . . ."

"He tried to force his attentions on her. I tell you, I *saw* it!" She insisted as Sam would have protested. "I'd have run him off the place, then and there, only Leora persuaded me you had enough to worry you, without knowing about that. So, against my better judgment I agreed he could stay—so long as he never tried anything of the sort again!"

Sweet, honest Leora! What Jane said made sense, however much he hated to accept it. Sam realized now there'd been a coolness between the two young people— that lately he hadn't seen them together, as he was used to doing. And this was why! The indignity of it filled him with a vast anger and made his voice shake a trifle as he said, between set jaws, "By God! I wish I had known!"

"You don't like what he did?" the woman countered, her chill look resting on him. "But is it any better to go tomcatting across the creek, with that blonde woman of Morgan Osgood's?"

She might as well have struck him. "You *believe* that? You think I was really the man?"

"How can I help but believe? I've seen what your brother is; and after all, you brought him here. No, Mister Cochran," and her eyes had surfaces of flint, "you'll oblige me very much if you both leave, and neither one of you come near T Square again!"

He could only stare. He thought he could almost feel the
105

pallor of his cheeks, and the weight in his chest was leaden. But if angry words welled upon his tongue, as he thought of all his selfless labors on behalf of the Tabbarts, he knew anything he might have said to this lonely and embittered woman would have been wrong; and so he merely shook his head and picked up the reins. He looked at the woman on the buckboard.

"You're the boss. Figure what you owe me and send it to the post office in town. I promise you've seen the last of the Cochrans!" And he pulled the black around, heading for the wagon to get his blanket roll. He went without a backward look for any of those who had hung back, to hear him fired from his job as foreman of the Tabbart brand.

CHAPTER XV

Before he left the field, there was one man he had to speak to. He spotted Irv Paley talking to a pair of his riders; as he was approaching, they left and Paley was alone when Sam came quartering up. The Hat owner turned in saddle to show him an impassive and expressionless face. Sam said, without any preliminary, "Irv, you're the last man I'd have thought would have any reason to stand up for me. I want to thank you."

The muddy, quarrelsome eyes revealed no softening. This man, who had given him so much trouble in the recent past, now merely shrugged; he seemed for a moment to have no intention of answering, but at last he spoke, grudgingly: "You're a man, Cochran—and by your lights, a fair one. Whatever my personal feelings, I didn't figure I could do any less."

Sam considered the answer, and the uncompromising scowl of the rancher's battered face. It was unlikely that these two could ever approach friendship, but at least they had learned a certain mutual respect. Sam left it at that. He nodded, and abruptly reining away lifted the black horse into a lope.

He could be grateful for one thing: Leora hadn't been there to hear the charges against him or to see Grif Storrs die. He knew she'd never believe the talk about himself and Sybil Osgood. There was going to be a real row between Leora and her mother over the firing of Sam Cochran, but argument wouldn't change Jane Tabbart's decision.

Jane, of course, had never felt he was a good enough man to stand in Bob Tabbart's shoes. Probably no foreman she was ever to hire would quite do, as the boss of the Tabbart brand. Even the truth about Sybil Osgood's affair with John Harnett, if and when it came out, wasn't likely to make any difference. She had formed her opinion of the Cochran brothers. She had seen Sam Cochran kill a man, even if by accident. Nothing anyone could say would change all that.

. . .

He rode on. Behind him branding fires were smoking; calves bawled and horses squealed and mounted men rode through the layers of hoof-raised dust, working the day's gather. Everything looked just as it had yesterday—and as it would tomorrow, without him. When he arrived at T Square headquarters and found the place deserted, he lost no time: He went directly to his living quarters, in the cubicle partitioned off at the end of the long bunkshack, and proceeded to collect his plunder.

He had never realized how stuff could accumulate, after a few years in one place and one job. Clothing and essentials offered no problem, it was the other things—the dog-eared magazines, the fishing pole, the French plaster doll he'd won once in a turkey shoot and never known what to do with. With a shake of his head, Sam rejected all this needless junk. Leaving it for the crew to divide or get rid of as they pleased, he stuffed his warbag with the bare necessities, carried it outside and strapped it behind the cantle with his blanket roll.

Then it was time to go. He stood a moment longer beside his horse, looking at this place that had been a home to him. Overhead the tall cottonwoods winked heliograph messages as the spring wind poured through their branches, and he could hear Leora's chickens clucking in their pen. He looked at the house and particularly at the window of Leora's room. A tug at his hatbrim, then, and he rose into the saddle; and that was the decisive moment. It marked the finish of his time here, closed out a chapter of his life. He slogged his boots into the stirrups and swung the black into the town trail, and he did not once let himself look back.

He was still some miles from the Colter Creek fording when his roiling thoughts made room for the awareness of someone else traveling this route; suddenly cautious, thinking of Reuben Choate or some other Clawhammer enemy, he pulled aside to wait, motionless, as that other horseman came up from behind him. There was the staccato roll of hoofbeats, approaching at an easy, steady rhythm;

then the claybank horse showed through the straight black trunks of the pines. The rider was his brother Mitch.

A hard mask dropped over Sam's blunt face, tightening his jaws until the muscles almost ached. Now the other had seen him. With a movement of pure surprise he hauled rein, so abruptly the claybank broke stride and tossed its head in a floundering stop. Mitch settled the animal. He said gruffly, "Well—hullo."

"You following me?" Sam demanded.

"No, just going the same place, I reckon. This *is* the town road, ain't it?" And as Sam nodded: "I just been to camp. I heard I'd been fired."

Sam said coldly, "It makes two of us."

"Heard that, too." Mitch seemed unsure of himself, uncertain just how to handle this. "I guess you felt kind of bad about it," he conceded, soberly; but then a cocky brashness twisted his mouth into a grin. "Oh, well. You're a good man, Sam. You can always find a place. I've found out, one job's about like another."

"And so is a woman?"

Something must have warned Mitch, then; the grin faded a trifle, the eyes became careful. "Maybe you'd like to chew that one a little finer. . . ."

Sam showed him a face like iron. "Is it true you had nerve enough to lay a hand on Leora Tabbart?"

There was a noticeable hesitation before Mitch answered the challenge with another. "Did she tell you some such yarn as that?"

"No. Her mother told me. And it wasn't a yarn."

"That old witch! Who'd believe *her*?" But the young fellow must have seen this line would get him nowhere, and so he backed water and conceded the point with a shrug. "Anyway, what the hell? Ain't like I hurt the girl none. . . ."

He lifted the reins, as though he had had enough of a pointless conversation. But a touch of Sam's knee put the black directly in his way, and Sam said coldly, "Get down off that saddle!"

Those other eyes hardened. "Why should I?"

Wasting no more breath on words, Sam simply booted his horse alongside the claybank and, before Mitch could guess what he was up to, reached and seized the younger man by an arm and by a handful of his shirtfront. In the next

109

moment, Mitch had been hauled bodily from his seat and was slammed on his back and shoulders in the road dust. As he lay there, dazed and surprised, Sam dismounted, batted the horses out of the way with a sweep of his hat, and afterward tossed the hat aside. His fists were balled as he stood over the fallen man.

He said tightly, "You're about to get the licking somebody should have given you, a long time ago!"

That brought the other to his feet. He had lost his own hat; the two of them stood bareheaded in the trail, half crouched, ready. "From you, big brother?" Mitch retorted. The cockiness was gone from his good-looking young face.

"I don't rightly know why I even bother with you!" Sam gritted. "I took you from the Denkers to try and save you from going bad. Now I begin to wonder if there's anything good in you at all!"

Listening, the younger man turned positively ugly. His eyes were slitted and the bunching of his cheeks pulled the upper lip away from his white teeth, in a look that was half a snarl. "By God, I can see you just been itching for this! Well, maybe you ain't quite as tough as you think you are!"

And Mitch charged.

These two had had their fights, in boyhood, when Sam with the advantage of his years had had to hold back something, while at the same time protecting himself from the full fury of the younger brother's rage. Now he knew he faced a different proposition; but he was still not quite prepared for the force of that first rush, or the weight of the fist that slammed him high on the forehead. Red flashes seared his vision and he felt himself giving ground. Then the instinct for self-preservation was at work and as the first numbing surprise passed, he raised a partial block against the next wild swing.

It struck his arm, skidded off the muscle of his shoulder, with force enough to remind him further that this was no youngster he faced but a man, with a man's hard, tough physique—in fact, that the difference in their years was now an actual advantage to the slim and wiry Mitch. After that Sam's boots were set in the tricky footing of the road ruts; he cocked a fist and let it explode directly in his brother's face. He felt it connect with a high cheekbone, the pain in his knuckles running all the way up his arm. And then his

110

brother's face fell away from before him and Mitch was on his back in the dirt.

He came bounding up again at once, apparently not at all hurt despite a smear of blood across his cheek, if anything he had been stung to greater fury. He came back at Sam, fairly leaping in to close the distance, but the older brother was ready for him. Fading back a step, he slammed Mitch in the chest and again in the face, batting aside the arm he raised to protect himself. Mitch swore, hoarsely, and then they were toe to toe, each trying to batter the other into the ground. In that kind of fighting, the older man's extra size and solid poundage in arms and shoulders carried the real advantage. But Mitch fought blindly. He was sweating like a horse, now, the breath whistling between drawn-back lips. And suddenly he was going down a second time, rolling, and Sam went after him, wading through a knee-high fog of dust.

He reached down into the dust, grabbed his brother's clothing and hauled him to his knees. Mitch swung, missed, and tried to grapple with him. Sam backed out of his arms and at the same time raised a bent knee against the side of the boy's head, twisting it violently to the side and sending him on his face in the dirt with arms spread wide.

There was no mercy in Sam, just then, as he grabbed him and pulled him up again. Mitch showed the punishment he was taking. Face battered and bleeding, his head lolled groggily as though his neck couldn't hold it upright; this alone stayed the fist that was set to smash him another time. Breathing heavily, Sam slowly lowered the arm. He shook his head and stepped back, letting Mitch go.

The young fellow sank back, catching himself there with his hands against the ground; head hanging, he muttered incoherently, "Enough—enough!"

Sam looked down at him, a long moment. "You positive?" He nodded then, heavily. "All right. . . ." He reached a hand to help the other up, but Mitch glared and flapped an elbow at him to keep him away. With shaky movements but under his own power, the young fellow got his knees under him and then his boots, and so came to his feet.

Watching, Sam touched the back of a hand to one nostril and looked at the dribble of blood. He said nothing as Mitch

111

beat ineffectually at the dirt clinging to his clothes, got his hat out of the road and pulled it on. The horses, on dragging reins, hadn't wandered far. Mitch walked unsteadily over to his claybank and took the leathers.

All the righteous anger that had been in Sam was dead, swamped under a rush of anguish and something very close to shame as he saw what his fists had done. He watched his brother swing stiffly into the saddle, and he felt he could hold it back no longer.

"Kid!" he exclaimed, and started forward. "Wait! Let me—" The words died under the impact of the bitter, hating stare that raked him. Without any answer, Mitch settled into the leather and kicked the claybank, hard.

Sam stood and watched him vanish into the timber that flanked the trail ahead, feeling like very hell.

Close to sunset Sam approached the wooden bridge over Colter Creek and, sending his horse down the bank there, dragged himself wearily off the saddle. Going down on his knees beside the bridge footing, he laid aside his hat and thrust both hands into swirling creek water. Its icy touch felt like fire where the skin was broken across the bruised and swollen knuckles. Sam winced, and proceeded to douse his face and head, running dripping palms down his cheeks and along the back of his neck.

Blowing water, he reached for neckcloth and dried his face, gingerly careful of the cut a wild swing of Mitch's fist had reopened, after it had barely healed from the mauling Grif Storrs gave him two weeks ago. He stayed that way a moment, looking at the peaceful reflection of red pine trunks that reached toward him across the moving water from the stand of trees and grass upon the farther bank. Feeling then that he at least looked a shade more presentable, he slicked back his wet hair with both palms, drew on his hat again, and pushed tiredly to his feet.

He rode across the bridge, the loose timbers rattling hollowly, and on into a town that was as quiet as he had ever seen it—for Sam, roundup was over, but for the rest of the Basin there was another half week to go. Still, he couldn't help a feeling as he rode up from the creek, into the crooked and dusty street with its silent double row of buildings, that knowing eyes were following his every move.

Somehow, he knew that word of what had happened at the Northern Division roundup camp was here ahead of him.

He faltered a moment approaching Harnett's office and held the black under taut rein a moment as he considered the blind, blank windows. But he shrugged and passed on. There was one thing he wanted, just now, and one place in town to get it. He rode directly to McLeod's.

A man sprawled in a chair on the saloon porch. It was Harv Boland, and like the first time Sam encountered him the gambler was asleep—uncallused hands limp in his lap, head tilted back against the wall, his snores enough to make one think he was strangling. He must find it a bore, Sam thought, waiting for Friday night when the crews would be in town at last, with roundup pay in their pockets and the need to throw it away in a boisterous letting off of steam.

On Friday, Harv Boland would be awake, all right—and more than ready to reap his share.

Sam entered the saloon. George McLeod, dealing solitaire in the quiet of the empty room, tossed aside the deck and got quickly to his feet, a look of concern on his honest face. "Sam!" he exclaimed. "I was hoping you'd come in."

Sam said bluntly, "Must mean you've heard the news."

"I've heard enough. Now I want *your* version."

"How about a shot of booze, first?"

"I'll have one with you." George went around behind the bar, brought up a bottle of his best stock. He scarcely had the glasses filled when Sam took his own and drained it off almost at a gulp. McLeod, thumbing the cork home, watched with disapproval as his friend shuddered and closed his eyes a moment. "Easy!" he exclaimed. "This stuff ain't water!"

"Never mind," Sam said gruffly. "And, damn it, don't go away with that!" He made a grab at the bottle and for a moment there was a contest of wills; then Sam shrugged and took his hand away. McLeod looked at him unhappily, and uncorking the bottle again poured Sam another bare half glass. This time Sam let it stand, while George stowed the bottle again below the counter.

McLeod said, "In your place I dunno but what I'd feel like taking on a load, myself; but, believe me, it don't solve

113

anything. You'll be a hell of a lot better off staying sober. Maybe you don't know it—but you're in danger!"

Sam shot him a look. "You think so?"

"You'd know so, if you'd of heard how Choate was talking when he came through town with Storrs's body! Clawhammer ain't gonna let this go, Sam. What you reckon to do about it?"

"I'm open to suggestions."

The saloonowner considered a moment before answering. "The first thing I'm willing to swear to," he said, "is that there's no truth to the story about you and Sybil Osgood. . . ."

That drew an oath from the other man. "Choate's even telling the world about *that*?"

McLeod nodded soberly. "He ain't exactly what you'd call a gentleman! As for what he's telling—well, I suppose I might believe some such thing of her, but never of *you*, Sam. And I'm thinking, if somehow we could learn the straight of it—"

"I know the straight of it."

McLeod stared. "You know the name of the man?" And at Sam's nod: "But—Good Lord! Can you get proof, somehow?"

"Beat it out of him, maybe?" Sam retorted. "And expect anyone to believe me?" He shook his head. "No, George, I'm not this man's conscience and I won't try to be. If he or Sybil Osgood want to come forward and own up to the truth, that's their business. I can't see it would make a lot of difference. It wouldn't bring Grif Storrs back to life!"

Frowning, McLeod said, "Still, I'm damned if I'd just hang around waiting until Osgood or some of his boys decide to even the score!"

"I'm beginning to wonder if there's any reason I should hang around, at all. Maybe you didn't know—I'm out of a job."

"No! Jane Tabbart fired you?"

"I more or less quit, actually; but I didn't have much choice. Anyhow, it wouldn't be right for T Square to get caught up in personal trouble between me and Osgood."

Soberly, the other nodded. "Yeah, I see that. . . . As for the job, you're too valuable a man to need to worry. There

114

ain't an outfit in the Basin wouldn't be more than happy to get you, once this thing with Clawhammer is settled."

Sam finished off his second drink, set the glass down and ran a palm across bruised and sore cheeks. "Might make more sense," he grunted, "was I to start over, somewhere else. . . ."

"The Basin's your home!" George McLeod objected. "You belong here. Give this time, Sam—it'll blow over." Impulsively he reached across the counter, laid a hand on his friend's arm. "Want some advice? Your trouble is you're dead on your feet. You've carried that job and that roundup on your shoulders until you didn't even know how worn out with them you really are. For tonight, don't even think about any of it. Go get yourself rest. In the morning, you'll have a clearer idea what to do."

Sam thought this over, convinced of its good sense. "All right, George." He started to reach for his pocketbook, but McLeod shook his head.

"Whisky was on the house. You know I always stand first drink, when roundup's over. You just jumped the gun a little." A nod and a grin thanked him. McLeod, watching his friend move toward the door, had a sudden thought that made him call out and hurry around the end of the bar, to join him there.

"In case you was thinking about the hotel—seems to me I wouldn't. That's the first place Clawhammer would look, if they had some notion you was in town." He added as Sam thought this over, frowning, "I got room in my stable for your bronc, and I reckon, at that, you'd find the hay in the mow a sight more comfortable than them broken-back beds at the hotel. Why don't you bed down there? Nobody'll know, and nobody can bother you."

The other man nodded. "Thanks. I might just do that." He pushed on out through the batwings, with another glance at Harv Boland who was still sprawled in his chair on the porch, chin sunk upon his breast.

Heading for the tie rail where his horse waited, he failed to see the glitter of the gambler's half-closed eyes watching him from behind a screen of lowered lashes.

Sunset—that time of day when any place at all looks at

115

its best—could almost transform the tawdry ugliness of the Denker spread. The flyblown window glass, and the flattened tins nailed over the worst of the holes in the roof, flashed with a borrowed brightness; the colors in the sky were copied in the turgid surface of the water tank. But dirt was dirt and trash was trash, and even the kindest of lighting effects couldn't disguise them.

Mitch Cochran saw only that smoke rose from the kitchen chimney and a lamp had already been lighted. As he pulled the claybank to a halt, uncertain about the reception he could expect, someone pushed open the screen door. It was Whitey Yates, the sometime Clawhammer rider, his strawcolored hair gleaming in long wings that fell on either side of a narrow face. He was muttering, "Now, who the hell's out here?" but when he saw Mitch, surprised recognition made his jaw sag. "Rupe!" he shouted across his shoulder. "Floyd! Come take a look. . . ."

Big Floyd came shouldering past, his healing arm wearing a bandage that was as grimily black as a piece of white cloth could get. His reaction was a harsh and suspicious oath. "Damn it, just what do you think you're up to? Ain't we had enough from you Cochrans?"

Mitch Cochran didn't have to answer the challenge. For old Rupe had come stumping out right behind the other two, humping along on that crutch of his; and Rupe must have read, in the visitor's face, that which lit his own in a grin of genial welcome. "Why, hell!" he exclaimed. "That's no way to talk to a youngster who's back where he belongs! Glad to see you, boy—right glad! Unload your saddle and bring your plunder in and join us. Floyd, deal out an extra plate.

"Old Uncle Rupe knowed you'd find your way back to us," he told Mitch pleasantly as the latter swung stiffly down, ignoring Floyd's scowl of suspicious dislike. "We knowed you knowed who your friends are. Step inside, lad. Make yourself to home. . . ."

CHAPTER XVI

Noon, to a gambler, was a more usual hour for rising; but on this particular morning Harv Boland was up and dressed and on the street almost before chill was out of the air. Anyone observing him must have sensed that he was intently waiting for something.

He prowled the street under a mood of high impatience, unable to stay in one place; his attention was divided between the silent facade of McLeod's, opposite, and the place where this street played out in the open sagebrush flats to southward. When at last a pair of riders shaped up there, coming out of the sage at a rolling jog, Boland turned instantly alert. He moved out to the edge of the boardwalk, to stand squinting in harsh morning light while he tried to determine who the new arrivals were.

They were Choate and Wiley, the Clawhammer riders; and recognition dried Boland's mouth and set his heart to pounding in nervous anticipation. He waited where he was, and the riders came on and pulled to a halt in front of him.

Big Reuben Choate looked down at the gambler, with a trace of contempt in his dark face. "All right," he said gruffly. "Where's he at?"

An instinct for the devious was at work in Harv Boland, even at such a moment as this. He sucked on a tooth as he said evasively, "Do I know who you're talking about?"

At that Choate slapped a callused palm against his saddlehorn and leaned forward to warn dangerously, "By God, don't get cagy with us! You sent word by one of our riders that Cochran was in town. You guaranteed he'd stay put and we could wait and pick him up this morning. Well, is he here, or ain't he? Because, if you've let him get away from us—"

"He's here!" Boland said quickly, all the studied poise

117

vanishing in the face of the threat. "Oh, he's here all right," he assured his questioners. "I been keeping watch, to make sure he didn't sneak out on you."

"Well? So where do we find him?"

Boland hesitated. He wet his lips while letting his glance roam the street nervously, wondering how well Choate's rumbling throat tones traveled, not pleased to advertise to the town what was afoot. "I'll show you."

"One thing I don't get," Neil Wiley said with a look of cold suspicion. "Just what the hell is in this for you?"

But how could he tell them? How could he explain the rankling resentment toward a stronger man—a man well liked and popular, with the friends and the standing that a jackleg gambler could never do more than envy? How even explain the humiliation of that morning when Sam Cochran invaded his hotel room and cuffed the pride and the courage out of him? Boland merely shrugged. "I got my reasons. If you want your man, come along. I'll lead you to him."

"Then do it!" Choate ordered, short-tempered and impatient.

Boland motioned with a jerk of his head and they followed him on across the street, at an angle, the horses' hoofs muffled by its thick dust. At this early hour the town lay quiet, and McLeod's saloon was shut down tight. There was a side alley beyond the corner of the big building; they took this, Harv Boland leading the way, and so approached the stable at the rear of the lot, past a stretch of weeds and trash and a pile of empty crates and bottles.

Through the doors that stood open on a dim interior, Sam Cochran was visible cinching the saddle onto his black gelding. He glanced around as their shadow came into the doorway; hastily then he backed clear of the animal.

The stable was a small one, only a couple of stalls on either side of a center aisle and a haymow over the rear. There was scarcely head room for a horseman to enter without dismounting, so Choate and Wiley slid off their saddles; when they strode inside Harv Boland was right behind them, to place his back against the rough pine boards next to the entrance. Looking at Sam Cochran's face, he was sweating suddenly, his breathing gone shallow and eager.

Cochran plainly knew he was in trouble; he faced the pair

118

from Clawhammer with a look of resignation, his shoulders rolled a trifle forward. So far no one had moved to touch a gun—Choate and his companion not needing to, their victim evidently aware it would be suicide to try. Reuben Choate broke the silence.

"It's another day, Cochran. I told you you hadn't seen the end of anything. Now we'll just pick up things where we left off—only, this time you got no friends to shove their noses in."

Neil Wiley said, "Yeah, you've run clean out of friends, mister!"

Sam Cochran asked, "Are you here to kill me?"

At the quietly spoken question Reuben Choate shook his head. "Nothing *that* crude! Anyway, it ain't our prerogative. We're just supposed to finish what Grif started to do yesterday. We're taking you to Morgan Osgood."

"And maybe you can believe," Wiley chimed in, "that he *really* wants to see you now, mister!"

Sam Cochran looked from one face to the other, as though weighing what they told him; and then his glance sought out Harv Boland, over against the door. His voice was more puzzled then accusing as he said, "You helped them find me, I guess. You must hate me more than I knew. . . ."

For some reason, under the weight of his stare, Boland was all at once uneasy—not quite so sure of this thing and of the satisfaction it gave him. He felt his face grow warm, and he retorted in a louder voice than he intended: "Whyn't you quit stallin', Cochran, and just go along with them? You know you got no choice."

Cochran looked again at Reuben Choate. "And if I won't?"

The big man's palm struck leather, and a Colt revolver pointed squarely at the prisoner's chest. "This says you will!"

"Even if you have to go against orders, and kill me?"

"I don't have to kill you." The gun barrel tilted slightly. "I can give it to you in a leg, or someplace equally painful, and take you in roped belly down to your saddle. You think you'd like that any better? It's your choice."

Sam Cochran appeared to consider the alternative, and

119

what he read in Choate's face must have convinced him the big fellow meant just what he said. With a shrug he turned to his saddled horse.

Neil Wiley cried: "Oh, no you don't!" His own gun was in his hand as he moved quickly toward Cochran. Harv Boland had no inkling of his intent before the blued gunbarrel rose and fell, in a chopping blow that clipped the side of the prisoner's skull, knocked the hat from his head and dropped him to hands and knees.

Standing over him as he crouched there with head hanging, Wiley shouted, "You're trying to make it too easy for yourself! You've walked tall around these parts, Mister Cochran, but that all ended when you killed Grif Storrs. Now, you *crawl* to that saddle! You hear me?" He leaned, snaked the gun from Cochran's holster, and putting a boot against the man's rump, drove him face-down into the filth of the stable floor. "*You crawl!*"

Only now, really, did Harv Boland understand just what he had done. A solid core of iron seemed to swell and harden in his chest, stopping his breathing, as his resentment of Sam Cochran was swamped and lost in sudden honor. He could only stand and watch Sam Cochran struggle up to his knees.

The prisoner was still dazed, probably, by that blow from the gunbarrel; perhaps he didn't even hear the command. But he went lurching forward, inching painfully toward the waiting horse; and his enemies went with him, standing directly over him and herding him on, allowing the dazed man no room or chance to regather his strength. When his shoulder touched the black's rear leg he stopped for a moment, as though uncertain what to do next. Big Choate cursed, at that, and swung a boot. Under the impact Sam Cochran swayed, but reached up and caught the stirrup and, using it to steady him, managed to set one boot under him. His head turned and Boland saw the shine of blood where that kick had laid his cheek open. His eyes, dulled with pain, rested on Boland's for a moment.

All at once, unable to stand this, Boland cried out and flung himself at Reuben Choate, clutching his arm as he exclaimed: "For the love of God! He's a man—can't you at least treat him like one?"

Choate turned long enough to snarl, in utter contempt,

"Shut up! You done yours. Now don't bother me!" A thrust of his arm sent the gambler stumbling, to slam helplessly against the wall and crumple there, staring dully.

With every sign of painful effort, Sam Cochran had pulled himself to his feet now and was trying to get a boot into the stirrup. Having made that, he put all his weight on the saddlehorn in the attempt to hoist himself astride. At his second try Choate must have lost patience with the game, for he reached suddenly, got a handful of the man's clothing and boosted him up. With this help Cochran got a leg across the saddle and somehow clung there. Choate picked up his hat and shoved it on his head for him; and after that Wiley took the black's reins and led it out to where the Clawhammer horses waited. Sam Cochran swayed in the saddle, doubled over the horn. His hunched shoulders cleared the low hang of the doorway by inches.

Harv Boland, huddled against the dark wall of the shed, heard all three horses swing into motion. The sound of their passage faded away down the alley, leaving him alone with his shame and the Judas-like knowledge of his degradation.

The Southern Division had been established hard by the broken foothill sector at the far end of the Basin, where the ringiest, toughest cattle were always to be found and gave the roundup crews their hardest battle. Coming in, the two Clawhammer riders and their prisoner smelled the dust and heard the bawl of the cattle before they were actually upon the camp.

They skirted the Osgood wagon and fire; as they passed the weather-stained army tent that Morg Osgood used for his headquarters, Sam Cochran had a glimpse—through the thrown-open canvas flap—of a cot with rumpled blankets, a folding chair and a deal table piled with tally books, a kerosene lantern hanging by its bail from the ridge pole. Osgood wasn't here, and they rode on with Reuben Choate and Neil Wiley searching the drift of dust and moving figures near the herd, hunting their boss.

Sam had had time to recover from the punishment inflicted by his captors' boots and Wiley's gunbarrel; he was able to sit the saddle and handle his own reins, and except for the cut on his cheek that had quit its bleeding and was scabbing over, he looked little the worse for that working-over in the barn. He rode docilely, not making any trouble. He could not escape, and he wouldn't beg. These men were, after all, only following orders. His fate lay with Morgan Osgood.

It was early, scarcely midmorning; most of the roundup crew would still be in the hills and draws, working on their gathers. But suddenly Neil Wiley spoke: "There's the chief." Choate saw, and with a grunt swung his bridles and pointed them in the new direction.

Morgan Osgood and a couple of his men were bringing in a bunch they had found somewhere up in the breaks. Nearly half were big two-year-olds, who didn't want to be driven and were tough enough and wild enough to give their handlers a bad time. Osgood was right in there, eating dust alongside his punchers, yelling and cursing and swinging a coiled rope in an effort to manage the intractable animals. Now he pulled aside and stepped down to lift and briefly examine the near front hoof of the big gray horse he rode, as though he thought it might be in danger of going lame. Straightening, through the drift of hoof-stirred dust he caught sight of Sam Cochran and seemed to forget every other thing.

You could almost see the way the thick chest swelled; Osgood appeared to grow inches taller than his actual solid bulk, and then his shoulders settled and his head sank forward, so that he was eyeing Sam Cochran from under a heavy shelf of bristling brows. As the horses were brought to a stand, Sam thought he could feel the fire of those staring eyes searing him.

A rumble stirred in Osgood's chest, became speech that shook with feeling. "So, you brought him!" he grunted to Reuben Choate, his eyes never leaving Sam's face. "Good work!" One arm lifted toward Sam, then, and the rope-hardened forefinger crooked in a peremptory, beckoning gesture.

Sam, not yet moving, felt a fist sharply prod his back and heard Choate's harsh command: "Get down."

Resignedly, he swung his boot over and dropped down into the dusty grass. The finger beckoned again and Sam walked toward Osgood. The two of them stood alone; Choate and Wiley, still mounted, watched from a little distance, while in the near background the punchers at the

122

herd whooped and pivoted their horses and fought with the tough-willed steers.

Osgood was perhaps a couple inches taller than the man he faced, and a good twenty pounds heavier—always an imposing figure, in saddle or afoot. Now he scowled at Sam Cochran, as from a pocket of his working vest he took one of the cigars he favored, bit off the end which he spat into the grass, and thrust the cigar between his jaws. He made no move to light it. Instead, he shook his massive head and remarked heavily, "I been fooled, on occasion. Not often, but sometimes pretty good. But I swear I never been so fooled by any man in my life, Cochran!" The unlighted cigar rolled between his meaty lips. Sam Cochran returned his look, determined not to show fear.

Osgood tried again. "I'm willing to hear anything you got to say for yourself, mister."

"On which count?" Sam asked.

The rancher gave a snort that fairly seemed to explode from his nostrils. "Yeah, I'll admit you got plenty to answer for, Cochran! My wife—and the best foreman I ever hired! By God, whatever you got to say I suggest you say it fast, while I'm in a mood to listen!"

"You won't believe me anyway," the other said with a shrug. "Just the same, whatever you may have been told was wrong. Killing Grif Storrs was an accident that I'd have done anything to avoid. All I can do is deny it."

The words were hardly spoken when Osgood's fist slammed him in the mouth, rocking his head upon his neck and mashing his lips and bringing the blood. His bootheel caught in a clump of bunch grass and only an awkward twist and lunge saved him from falling. Across the little distance that separated them, Morgan Osgood's fury flared at him. "By God, I guess there ain't anything you won't do—or any lie you won't tell to try and save your stinking hide!"

In back of Sam, somebody—either Choate or Wiley— laughed scornfully. Sam touched tongue to the split lip, tasted the iron tang of blood. He said in a dull voice, "If you're determined to have me a liar, Morg, then there's no use my saying anything."

The fist that had struck him opened and closed as Osgood worked the fingers, and Sam waited half expecting it to smash him again. Over in the drift of dust surrounding the herd a rider yelled something, like a warning, but Osgood seemed neither to hear nor heed. He said roughly, "Is that the best you can do? Because, it's pretty damn poor. . . ."

The cowboy shouted again, in even sharper warning. It dragged Sam's stare past Osgood, and then his eyes widened and he was trying to speak but no sound came from him. Morgan Osgood, for his part, sensed or heard something that made him jerk about—just in time to meet the charge as a huge brute of a steer came bursting out of the dust cloud with head lowered, tongue dangling redly, wicked horns glinting.

Sam, himself equally in danger, managed a backpedaling lunge that carried him out of its path; Osgood's gray saddle horse trumpeted in alarm and swerved clear. But the man was both too slow and too clumsy. He met the rush head on, big hands coming up as though he hoped to seize those wicked horns and deflect them. Man and steer collided with an audible smash, and Osgood was picked bodily from the ground, lifted and thrown across one strongly muscled shoulder. He hit the earth in a rolling sprawl. The beast lunged on.

Choate and Wiley were both yelling, insanely and futilely. Sam Cochran stood rooted, staring at the limp shape that looked like nothing more human than a pile of old clothing. From somewhere a rider came spurring, yelling and flipping his coiled rope as he circled to head off the animal that had thrown the Clawhammer boss; the steer, really in a frenzy now, braked to a halt. It stared at the horseman, swung its massive head and the horns one of whose tips was reddened now. It swerved, swapped ends in no space at all and was lumbering off again on knife-sharp hoofs.

Sam Cochran, recovering from his first frozen shock, was moving numbly toward Osgood's unmoving shape when he heard the nearing pound, and jerked his head about. At the same instant the steer sighted the man it had thrown and some instinct to kill made it swerve in Osgood's direction, its head lowered and horns ready to hook and gore. There was a leeway of no more than seconds; and Sam moved with a quickness he had never known he possessed.

It was the dull gleam of the gun in Osgood's holster that

drew him. Three strides brought him to the downed man's side; a lunge dropped him to his knees while his hand reached for the gun, slid it clear. A blind thrust lifted it, swinging on the lunging target. The steer was so close that he could not have missed the target of the massive skull—so close that Sam almost thought he felt the warmth of the snorting breath that, with every lunge, erupted puffs of dust from the earth beneath the brute's flaring nostrils.

He fired, twice, as fast as he could work the trigger. The steer halted as though it had struck a wall. The head went down; the horns rammed earth, dug deep, and the heavy body somersaulted. The very ground seemed to shake as it landed, less than a yard from Sam Cochran's kneeling figure and from the man who lay—still and bleeding—in the dirt beside him.

CHAPTER XVII

After that, everything seemed to stop.

Sam Cochran was still numbed and dazed by the suddenness of what had happened. As the dust and fog of burnt powder sifted and scattered, he sank back upon his ankles and lifted a hand to wipe the palm shakily across his face; he looked at Morgan Osgood, then, and saw the movement of uneven breathing, and the spreading stain of blood. When he lifted his head, he saw that other riders gathered but like Choate and Wiley they merely sat their saddles, staring dumbly.

If Grif Storrs had been here to take command, they would no doubt behave differently. But Storrs was dead, and with Osgood stricken these Clawhammer riders were men without a leader. And Sam Cochran, his temper slipping, heard himself shout at them as he came up to his feet: "What's the matter with you, anyway? The lot of you going to just let him lie here and bleed to death? Do something!"

Reuben Choate said gruffly, "He ain't dead?"

"He sure as hell will be, if someone doesn't get busy—and quick!" Almost without knowing it, Sam found he had taken charge; and in the way of dazed and leaderless men, they were letting him. "One of you get into town and fetch the doctor back with you, fast as you can make tracks. Somebody else, bring that cot from the tent—we can use it to carry him over there and make him easy as possible until Harnett arrives."

Being given something to do snapped them out of their shock. Neil Wiley said quickly, "I'll find the doc," and was gone at once, whipping up his horse in the direction of town. A second rider went spurring toward the tent; the others hastily dismounted to gather in a silent knot and stare at the injured man.

"Stay back!" Sam warned. "Don't crowd him! Hold a hat over his face, somebody—keep the sun glare off. One of you, catch up his horse. And I guess, while we're at it, somebody ought to get word to Mrs. Osgood of what's happened. . . ." That seemed to take care of as much as he could think of at the moment.

He saw Reuben Choate scowling at him, but the man turned away without saying anything as the rider came galloping back from the tent, with the folding cot balanced across his saddle. While Osgood was being carefully and gingerly lifted onto it, suddenly Sam realized he still held the sixshooter he had taken from the hurt man's belt to kill the steer. He hesitated, then dropped the weapon into his own empty holster.

So far no one appeared interested in trying to take it away from him. No one, not even Reuben Choate, seemed to remember he was a prisoner. . . .

Neil Wiley, luckily enough, appeared to have had no trouble locating John Harnett. When he returned, accompanied by the doctor, the initial confusion over the accident to Morgan Osgood had barely had time to settle. Riders coming in off the circle and learning the news had helped to keep the excitement alive; roundup was forgotten and now men were standing around, the inevitable tin cups of coffee in their hands, keeping vigil.

Whether or not a man liked the Clawhammer boss, he was one who commanded respect. And now he lay on the cot inside the tent, out of his head with the pain of a gored abdomen, calling feverishly for water which Sam Cochran would allow to be given him only sparingly—until they knew how severe his hurt really was, it wasn't safe for him actually to be allowed anything to drink.

Ducking into the tent, clutching his black leather bag in the hand he raised to push aside the flap, Harnett straightened and halted as he came face to face with Sam Cochran; they eyed each other for a long moment, in the breathless heat and muted light concentrated beneath the sloping canvas roof. Harnett was the first one to break gaze, and from that Sam was sure he knew the circumstances of Morgan Osgood's injury, and had probably been able to guess at the part that wasn't general knowledge.

Harnett shifted his glance to the man on the cot, and Sam explained coldly, "Steer hooked him, just under the ribs—I don't know how bad, or how deep. The cook gave me some clean dishtowels and I've been using them, trying to keep the blood soaked up. He's lost a sight of it."

Edging aside in the cramped space, he made room for Harnett to step to the cot and place his bag on the crude deal table. Harnett carefully removed the blood-soaked compress, examined the wound with an impartial, critical look that told nothing. "All right," he said brusquely. "I'll take over."

Though he had been dismissed, Sam made no move as yet to go. Harnett, doffing his coat and starting to roll his shirtsleeves, couldn't ignore that other presence. He turned, frowning, a breath swelling his chest.

"Look! I heard how it happened. It's the second time you've taken punishment for me. I'm not proud of it. And I know what you must be feeling."

"I doubt that!" Sam retorted. He added bluntly, "Mostly what I feel right now is disgust—that a man as intelligent as you are could go right on making the same damned mistake after he should have learned better."

Color tinged the lean cheeks; Harnett's head lifted sharply. In the heat of the tent, beads of moisture stood along the prematurely graying temples. "I never asked you to cover for me! Why don't you go right ahead—tell all of them the truth?"

"Why don't *you*?" Sam challenged him. He didn't expect, or get, an answer; no man could be expected openly to admit to the limits of his courage. Changing the subject, he indicated the unconscious figure on the cot. "Can you save him?"

"That's hard to say. I'll do my best."

"You'd better!" The sudden sharpness of the words held the other's stare as Sam moved to the tent opening.

Unable to hold it back, Harnett flung his question after him. "What did you mean by that?"

Sam turned; his glance was cold with warning. "The man's life is in your hands. It's surely occurred to you that, if he dies, it can mean your chance at his widow, and Clawhammer, and every other damn thing that goes with her. All you need to do is forget, just for a minute, that you're a doctor." He nodded bleakly. "Yeah, it might be tempting. . . ."

John Harnett's voice ripped at him like the edge of a file. "Get out of here!"

A final, judging look, and Sam turned away. He ducked out through the flap.

The breeze felt cold against his cheeks, and the colors of everything seemed odd to eyes grown accustomed to that drab half-light beneath the canvas. He thought again, blinking into the brilliant sunglare, that it was amazing how he had been allowed to take charge of things when, less than an hour ago, he had been a prisoner in this roundup camp. Even Choate seemed disinclined to make any move against him. Choate, he decided, was a man who needed someone else to give him his orders. But even so, and even with a gun in his holster, he wouldn't try to guess what Choate would do if he were to try to leave.

For the time being things were in John Harnett's lap, and a reaction hit Sam Cochran suddenly, turning him weak-kneed and shaking. He began to realize he had had no breakfast, so he wandered over to the cookfire and helped himself to coffee from the smoke-blackened pot. The cook silently handed him a plate of beans and dutch-oven biscuits; Sam thanked the man with a nod, and found a place to sit crosslegged and have his meal.

He was spooning the last of the molasses when a shadow fell across him. A rider loomed above him. Sam's head lifted, an astonished glance moving up the claybank's muscled flank, on up the denimed leg of the man in the saddle until it reached the rider's face; and there it stopped, in disbelief. For the rider was his brother Mitch, and for a moment Sam could only stare, simply unable to understand his presence.

Mitch looked bad this morning. His face was swollen and bruised, one cheek puffed out in such a way that the eye

129

above it was nearly shut and couched in discolored, angry-looking flesh. It gave him a sinister cast, and the sullen set to his mouth didn't help—nor did the knowledge that it was Sam's own fists that had done this to him.

"What are you doing here?" Sam demanded roughly.

Mitch glanced around and seemed to see too many curious and watching eyes to please him. He made a summoning motion with his head, and pulled his horse around and rode away a few yards, obviously expecting Sam to follow. The latter hesitated, then with a puzzled scowl laid plate and cup aside and got to his feet.

His brother had swung down from the saddle and was standing, holding the reins. "You looking for me?" Sam wanted to know. "And how the hell did you know where to find me?"

"I ran into Harv Boland, in town. . . ."

"Oh." Sam made a sour face. "Your tinhorn friend! Yeah, he could have told you, I guess!"

The young fellow colored slightly. "All right, he ain't much! He admitted he was the one turned you over to Morg Osgood's men. Fact is, he's damn well broke up about it. You can believe that if you want to," he added belligerently, as he saw his brother's skeptical look. "It's nothing to me!"

"Maybe," Sam replied gruffly, "I'm supposed to believe you came out here to try and save my neck?"

"Supposing I did?" Mitch countered, his hostility matching Sam's. "From all I see here, looks like you ain't in much trouble; I needn't have wasted my time. Well, I never was too bright!"

"Hold on!" Sam exclaimed as the other started to turn away. Mitch gave him a smoldering look. "You really mean it, don't you? That's really why you came. . . ."

"Well, that was part of it. I had something to tell you—

Sam said quietly, "I'll listen."

Sam said qietly, "I'll listen."

So the young man shrugged and told it, almost grudgingly: "Yesterday, when you got done beating the custard out of me, I went right straight to the Denkers. Sure—why not?" he challenged as Sam's eyes went hard. "It was one way I could think of to hurt you—and that was the one thing I wanted to do."

"Your friends glad to see you?" Sam was coldly sarcastic.

"Damn right! I fit right in with something they'd been planning and needed help with. You want to hear it, or not?"

"Keep talking. . . ."

"It's that bunch of stock T Square's been gathering for shipment. Rupe and Floyd have had their eye on it, a good piece now. They even got a buyer ready to take it off their hands—all they have to do is run the stuff into the hills and deliver it. Long as you was foreman, they never had nerve to try; but now they figure is their chance."

"Now?" Sam repeated sharply. "You mean—*today*?"

"I reckon they're on their way right this minute. They wanted me along, but I told them I wouldn't have any part of it."

"Why not?"

Mitch echoed the question in a voice that was hoarse with anger: "Why not! You just won't give me a thing, will you? Even if I had the makings of a cow thief, I couldn't steal from a brand I'd ridden for—not even the Tabbarts'! And I couldn't stand by and see it done, either."

"But why tell *me* about it? Why not go to Vic Bonner? Or Jane Tabbart, herself?"

Mitch colored angrily. "Why should I do that old battleaxe any favors?" he retorted; but then his stare slid away from his brother's. He shrugged. "Forget it. For some reason, I thought you might feel the same as I did."

Sam understood then. "You want to *do* something about this, kid? Is that it?"

The eyes lifted, met his defiantly. "Do you?"

A moment, then Sam nodded. "I'll get my bronc. . . ."

The black gelding had been caught up and tied to a wheel of the chuck wagon. He jerked the reins free and was just settling into the saddle when a yell from Reuben Choate brought his head around. Choate was running toward him, across the trampled grass. "Cochran!" he shouted—and then hauled up short as Sam showed him the gun from his holster.

"Don't interfere with me, Choate!" Sam warned, in a voice of iron. "I'll settle my business with Morg Osgood, in due time, but I've had all from you I'm going to take. Now, stand back!"

Members of the Southern Division stood watching from

131

the sidelines, no one offering Choate any help; and now even he seemed to lose his eagerness. His shoulders settled; his stare wavered and dropped to the ground at his feet. And Sam Cochran, sliding the gun back into holster, pulled the black around to join his brother who was already mounted and waiting for him.

Dry dust spurted under their horses' hoofs as they left the roundup camp behind them—the fires and the wagons and the herd, and that tent where John Harnett was alone with his patient. At the very edge of the flats, Sam saw a single rider approaching. Within minutes he could identify the figure on the sidesaddle of the strawberry roan, and his look turned bleak as he wondered what Sybil Osgood would have to say to him, and what answer he would make.

But when they met, she neither halted nor offered him so much as a glance. Eyes set straight ahead in her pale, cold face, she rode past as though he hadn't been there at all. And Sam lifted his shoulders slightly and spurred on, satisfied to leave matters so.

Mitch exclaimed sharply, "What the hell! Wasn't that Osgood's wife?"

Sam merely nodded. He had more important things than Sybil Osgood to worry about, just then. . . .

The Northern Division hadn't moved from yesterday's encampment, east of Ryan's Creek. Hard pressed by a sense of urgency, the Cochran brothers found to their sharp disappointment that the holding ground appeared all but deserted. They made for the Tabbart wagon, where Smitty, the cook, was busy at his tailgate worktable mixing up a batch of biscuits for the dutch oven. Arms white to the elbows with flour, Smitty stared.

"You two! I never expected to see either one of you again!"

"Where is everybody?" Sam demanded impatiently, while the black danced around under him, feeling its rider's impatience.

"Out on circle," the cook answered. He explained: "We got off to a late start here, this morning—things in general been kind of discombobulated ever since you left. After some wrangling, Red Steens finally took over running the Division and giving out the day orders."

"You happen to know what area T Square is working?"

Smitty wiped his hands in his apron, plainly intrigued and alarmed by Sam Cochran's manner. "Over toward the Little Brothers, I think. Back in them draws beyond there."

Sam swore under his breath. Mitch, looking at his brother, demanded, "Not enough time to reach them, huh?"

"Not near enough. We'll have to do the best we can without."

He was already lifting the reins, prodded by the wastage of time. Seeing the pair about to leave, Smitty cried anxiously, "Wait a minute! What the hell's going on, Sam?"

Mitch was the one who reined in long enough to fling him his answer: "In case anyone really wants to know, the Cochran brothers are about to risk their stupid necks to keep the Denkers from grabbing off that T Square shipping herd—after T Square pitched us both to the dogs!"

"Let it go, kid!" Sam grunted, and gave his horse the boot. Mitch had to do the same to overtake the quick lunging lead he took. As they spurted away, they left a thoroughly troubled cook staring after them.

"What's your guess?" Sam asked when they had pressed on a while in silence. "How many are we up against?"

Mitch made careful answer. "In addition to Floyd and Uncle Rupe, the only one I saw was Whitey Yates—"

"Yates! Is *he* still around?" Sam muttered sourly, remembering the Clawhammer rider who'd sold out Sybil Osgood to the Denkers, for the hope of sharing with the Denkers in a ransom payoff. "I thought he left this country."

"If he did he's back. And he may have brought a couple more with him. At least I heard mention of somebody named McKay and somebody named Gaffey. I got an idea they're expected in time to help with the job."

"Five," Sam muttered. "How are you for that kind of odds?"

Mitch shrugged. "They'll do, for want of any better." He sounded reckless and indifferent, but Sam had a feeling the young fellow secretly shared his own half-scared determination. In that moment he felt closer to Mitch than at any time he could remember since boyhood. Seemed like hell, that it took something like this to do it.

Neither of them said much, after that, until they reached

133

the meadow where the shipping herd ought to have been. They had known they would find nothing, and they were right. The meadow was empty. But as they rode slowly across the trampled grass, sign of the missing cattle was easy enough to trace, and the prints of the horses belonging to the men who had driven them off.

There was no way to conceal the passage of two or three hundred head of beef, and the Denkers hadn't tried. Mitch Cochran drew alongside his brother's stirrup while he pointed excitedly ahead. "Straight up that slope—where them aspens spill out of the draw."

Sam nodded. "It's the quickest route into the timber. But I doubt they'll have more than an hour or so on us, and even five men won't make time pushing cattle through that kind of country. I reckon we'll hang with it, a while."

"I'm game," Mitch agreed promptly enough.

CHAPTER XVIII

John Harnett pushed aside the tent flap and came out blinking in the sunshine, coat slung across his arm. He felt old, used-up. His shirt clung to him, drenched in sweat; pausing to finish rolling down a shirtsleeve and fumble with the cuff-stud, he saw Sybil Osgood just getting up from the wooden box someone had fetched her for a seat. He felt her eyes on him.

Men stood about, intently watching, but they kept a respectful distance as Sybil walked over to the tent, smoothing the hang of her long, full skirt with nervous strokes of her hands. She looked up into Harnett's face and her look spoke her question. Slowly, he nodded.

"You can see your husband now, Mrs. Osgood," he said, speaking to some point above the woman's head. He shrugged into his coat, his movements infinitely weary. "It was as difficult a piece of work as I have ever faced. For a while, I wasn't sure I was going to be able to bring it off."

"You mean—he's going to *live*?"

"For a wonder! That steer's horn missed the vital organs, though it did damage enough. He's lost a terrifying amount of blood. But—yes, Morgan Osgood will live."

Her expression changed. Her eyes narrowed and her mouth drew out long. "Oh, you fool!" she whispered, fiercely. "Why didn't you let him die? That was a chance we might never have again. It would have solved every one of our problems—and nobody in the world could ever blame you."

"Nobody," he agreed in the same dead tone. "Except myself. . . ."

"You don't even make sense!"

John Harnett looked at her, almost as though for the first time with eyes that saw her clearly. "It's the only sense I've made in the months since we started this affair," he said. "And no credit to me: All the time I was working on him

135

something that fellow Cochran told me was going through my head. 'Try to remember,' he said, 'that you're supposed to be a doctor!' And do you know, somehow I couldn't think of anything else!"

The breath hissed between her teeth. "So now you're making Sam Cochran your conscience?"

"It might be well," he answered coldly, "if you were to try remembering for once that you're a wife! You understand, Morgan Osgood's going to be an invalid—for some time to come. He'll need someone waiting on him, night and day. I'm afraid it looks like your job."

"And—you and me? That means nothing any more?"

"It never could have meant anything," John Harnett said. "So why don't we admit it? Your husband's awake," he went on, as Sybil merely stared at him from a face gone white as bone. "He's asking for you. I've told him the whole truth about the two of us—he already knew your part, but he thought it was Cochran instead of me. . . . For now, I'd suggest you keep him just where he is. Perhaps tomorrow, it will be safe to move him to the ranch. I'll be out to help with that."

Sybil Osgood's breast swelled, her hands clenched. There was nothing beautiful about her, now. "You can stay away, Doctor Harnett. I don't need you. I never want to see you again! Do you understand?" She repeated it, her voice rising: "I said, do you understand me—you filth?"

But John Harnett had turned away, with a brief touch of forefinger to hatbrim, and was walking toward his waiting horse. His face was expressionless, fending off the covert glances of the Osgood riders. Behind him the woman's voice, unheeded, rose to a screech and broke and ended in a sob of fury.

He did not once look back.

The Cochran brothers first heard the bawling protest of cattle being driven when they stopped a moment to rest their horses. They had known they must be close—very close indeed—but the sounds of their own travel, and the heavy labored breathing of their own animals, covered any rumor of movement ahead of them. It was miserable country for traveling, steep and timbered. The horses made heavy going of it. And the solid ranks of pine that crowded the trail, already showing signs of giving place to fir as the way

136

climbed higher, probably helped sop up a lot of the sound that might have warned them.

Now, as the horses blew under them, Mitch flung up a hand and Sam nodded quickly, already listening to the message that a cold wind, flowing down into their faces, carried with it. "There it is!" the younger man grunted, and his voice sounded a trifle shaky with tension.

Sam's own throat felt dry. He saw his brother fumble at the gun in his holster and said quickly, "We won't do anything foolish. Remember, there's five of them. We got an advantage, in that they probably don't know we're on top of them. Let's keep it that way while we can. . . ."

The trail had grown so fresh they could all but see the trampled clumps of bunch grass uncurling, and Sam thought he could smell raised dust and hoof-stirred forest litter. The sound of moving cattle came intermittently now, and twice a rider's faint yell reached through the stillness. The way skirted a fan of talus rubble that had sometime or other spilled down from a broken rim, knocking over trees as it fell; as they worked past this tangle of rock and down timber, a sloping meadow opened ahead and there, suddenly, was the last tail-end of the drag, just merging into the timber beyond. A rider on a brown horse swung his coiled lass rope and hurried them on.

This man was a stranger to Sam, who decided he must be either McKay or Gaffey—one of the new recruits to the Denker outfit, that Mitch Cochran had heard mention of. Whoever it was, he had the double job of keeping up the drag, while at the same time maintaining a watch over the back trail; and now apparently he'd caught some warning movement in the screen of alders, at the foot of the meadow. For all at once he whipped about, shifting his rope to his left hand while with his right he fumbled at a belt holster.

It was a long reach for accurate shooting. Sam swore and drew his gun, saying, "We got to stop him, before he alerts the others!" The rider must have had the same thought. He seemed to give up the idea of using his own weapon and instead was yanking his mount's head around, as though to boot him into the upward timber.

Sam was debating whether to risk a shot, that would likely miss and carry its own warning, when beside him Mitch reached some decision of his own. Before the older man could make a move to stop him, he clapped spurs to flanks and sent the claybank lunging straight forward, out into the open. And Sam held his breath as that other rider saw and swung back again, sunlight flashing now from a gunbarrel.

Mitch rode toward the man, unhurriedly; his own gun was still in its holster. The rustler halted him while he was still some ten yards distant, projecting his warning above that last bawling straggle of cattle: "Don't come any closer!"

His words reached clearly to Sam, who had held up behind the screen of alders to watch whatever might develop. "Who are you, anyway? What the hell do you think you want?"

"Why, I'm Mitch Cochran," the boy answered, calmly enough, though he had obligingly pulled in his horse. "Reckon you'd be Roy Gaffey."

Gaffey didn't bother to deny it. His voice held its original freight of suspicion. "You got no business here! What I heard, you backed out on this operation."

"Maybe I changed my mind again. From what I see, looks like you could use some help."

"Who's with you? Didn't I just see a second rider, down in them alders?"

"Dunno what could make you think that," Mitch lied smoothly. "I came alone. . . . Look, let me talk to Rupe Denker—okay? He'll tell you I'm all right. Come on, mister! How about it?" He was turning all his smooth charm on the man, and it apparently had Gaffey undecided. And taking advantage of this, Mitch turned away suddenly to yell at a steer that had dropped behind and looked ready to bolt the tail end of the herd.

He spurred his horse, got the animal headed and pushed him back into the drag; the other man, reminded that he was neglecting his work, cursed and went charging after another of the lagging steers. Sam Cochran, watching from the alders, had to admire the smoothness with which his brother had got around the outlaw, even while he wondered what the boy had in mind to do next.

He learned, an instant later.

A swerve of his claybank had brought Mitch close to the other rider, and just a shade behind him. Gaffey had his attention taken and didn't seem to sense the danger; and though it was only for a moment, it was long enough. Sam saw Mitch's arm lift and fall, saw the winking streak of the gunbarrel descending. The hat popped from Gaffey's head and he crumpled, driven from saddle.

Sam winced as the blow landed, but he was already kicking his horse into the open. Mitch had reined in briefly to take a look at the man he had felled—a motionless huddle, now, on the sparse soil of the slope. And this was the tableau in front of Sam when, lifting his head sharply, he saw another rider emerging from the trees.

It was Whitey Yates—no mistaking the pale shine of the blond hair that hung in wings below the brim of his battered hat. He had appeared in time to see Gaffey go down under the clubbing stroke of Mitch Cochran's gunbarrel. At once he yanked to a halt and the long tube of a carbine slid from his saddle scabbard and leveled on young Cochran.

Barely in range, Sam cried out and fired, his shot going wild; but at least it deflected the blond man's attention from Mitch. The carbine barrel swung to meet the new challenge. Still galloping ahead, Sam fired again and this time he didn't miss. His bullet struck, and the kick of the rifle, exploding harmlessly, helped to knock the renegade Clawhammer rider backward across his horse's rump.

Belatedly, Mitch Cochran saw the peril he'd been in. He could only stare as the older brother raced past, gesturing with his smoking gun. "Come on!" Sam yelled at him. "We only got seconds, now the shooting's begun!"

Whitey Yates's frightened horse skittered out of his path and he saw Whitey—alive, on his back and moaning with pain. Sam's bullet had struck the man in the hip, and there was blood enough to make him gag a little; he looked resolutely away, swallowing convulsively and tightening his hand on the gun. He told himself the thing that mattered was that Yates and Gaffey were both out of the fight. That left three.

Mitch had been lost somewhere behind him now and there wasn't time to look for him. Sam overtook the rear of the moving herd, and cattle scattered around him as he came into the timber where hoof-raised dust drifted thickly among the straight, tall trunks. He pushed on, hunting nervously, knowing full well that the spatter of gunfire would have carried forward and that undoubtedly the Denkers knew by now of the trouble at their rear.

Suddenly a revolver shot lashed flatly above the bawling

of the herd, and bark exploded from a treetrunk close beside his cheek. Sam swayed away from it, and caught a glimpse of Uncle Rupe Denker, huddled in the saddle with his homemade wooden crutch lashed to the saddlestrings. With too much haste, Sam worked the trigger and knew he missed. Rupe Denker's horse drifted on somewhere through the tawny fog of dust, and was gone again from sight.

Sweat broke out on Sam Cochran. Surrounded by bawling cattle, he realized he was alone and trapped, unable to move in any direction as they jostled his frightened horse and angry-looking horns clashed and glinted dangerously close beside his stirrups. He would make a fine target for anyone who happened to come upon him here! Spurred by the thought, he swung his sixgun over and down and fired directly into the earth, off his left stirrup.

Cattle bellowed in terror at the flash and roar of the weapon, and those nearest bucked away from him, climbing over one another in their frantic efforts to get clear. The black was trembling in every limb but Sam kicked him hard as, yelling hoarsely, he fired again and yet a third time into the very faces of the animals. Eyes rolled whitely and fear distended the bawling throats; constantly pressing, Sam all at once found himself in the open, at the edge of the swarm of red backs and gleaming horns.

The choking dust fell away slightly and he could breathe. One leg of his jeans was ripped and bloody but he scarcely noticed the fiery streak of pain. He was hunting blindly through the trees, listening but hearing nothing of his enemies, almost able to imagine he was all alone here, with this bawling scatter of terrified cattle. . . . He remembered that the gun in his own hand—the one he'd taken from Morgan Osgood's holster—would be nearly empty, and he rolled the cylinder out and with numb fingers punched the empties and fed in fresh shells from his own belt loops, dropping a couple in his fumbling haste.

All at once there wasn't time to finish that job. He slapped the cylinder back into place with a swipe of his palm, and twisted in the saddle as Floyd Denker and another man loomed blackly out of the fog of dust.

Big Floyd still carried his injured arm in a sling, but that left hand was able to manage the reins, holding them tight against his thick chest, while his right held his Winchester— stock clamped under elbow, muzzle pointed at Sam like a lance. The rider with him would be the second addition to the crew, the one named McKay—a mere blur to Sam, just now, in the dust and the nerve-tightening excitement of the moment. They both must have been riding at point, pushing the head of that stream of stolen cattle; would have been the last to hear the shooting and become aware something was happening at the tail of the drive. Now they were coming, straight at Sam Cochran.

He held his ground and with jaws clamped made himself pick a target—the place where the dirty cloth of the sling crossed Floyd's thick chest. The Winchester bloomed with muzzle-flame but the man was coming on too fast for accurate shooting. Sam made himself face it without flinching. Deliberately, then, he threw off his own shot and saw Floyd sway in the saddle.

The big fellow dropped his smoking rifle, grabbing at the horn to right himself. With dogged will he reached for his left gun, actually got his hand on it and was pawing it up out of the leather, when Sam shot again. The reports mingled in shocking concussion and a cloud of acrid smoke. Floyd Denker tumbled headlong from the saddle.

He was the first man Sam had ever deliberately killed, but there was no time to think of that. Instead he whirled the black and spurred directly at the man named McKay, who had a gun in his hand but was making no move to use it. "Throw it away!"

The man merely looked at him, and at the smoking gun leveled at him. He was an unimpressive sort, with sandy hair and a straggling droop of mustache that only made his face look weaker. With a contemptuous movement, Sam reached and picked the sixshooter out of his fingers and flung it aside.

"Don't kill me!"

Sam ignored the hoarse and frenzied plea. Letting him have the full effect of the gun's muzzle pointed at his face, he demanded sharply, "How about it? There any more of you?" But the fellow was too terrified to speak; even his head shook in spasms on the end of his neck. Sam dismissed him as of no importance at all.

Floyd Denker he didn't look at again knowing the man was dead. He peered about through the drift of dust that was thinning now as the last of the cattle scattered and vanished into the timber. He was wondering, What of Mitch, and ·

Uncle Rupe? And no sooner had he framed the question than he heard the answer, in a flurry of shooting that broke, suddenly, somewhere downwind from him.

Sam Cochran swore aloud and wrenched his horse about with a yank at the reins. He started to use the rowels, then as quickly curbed the black down again so that it tried to rear, shaking its head at such unaccustomed treatment. That was something Sam couldn't help; it was only now he had heard the other horse approaching—bearing in from the sector where he had heard the gunfire, coming at a shambling run.

He waited, tense as a drawn bow, and a moment later the horse and its rider showed through the lower trees. The man was Rupe Denker. He had lost his hat and the thinning hair stood fiercely upon his skull. Clutching the big hogleg revolver, he had the wildest look Sam had ever seen on a man. And when he saw Sam his whole body seemed to jerk and let out an almost inhuman screech: "You damned Cochrans! Is it up to me to kill *all* of you?"

Sam's gun settled on the man, even as a leaden weight formed inside him at the word that Mitch was dead. But he didn't use the gun, for suddenly Rupe wasn't even looking in his direction. The old man's shoulders hunched, his head lowered. He let the heavy revolver fall and one clawlike hand went to his chest, as something shook him convulsively. A sudden gout of blood flowed from his mouth; his body turned shapeless and slack. When he slid from the saddle, one limp shoulder struck a pine trunk and his clothing scraped bark as he went down.

Sam Cochran drew a shuddering breath and tore his eyes at last from the old man's lifeless body. Well, he thought grimly, if he had done for Mitch, at least the boy had made him pay the price. Sam looked over at McKay, who hadn't stirred in his saddle; the man lifted a sickly and pallid face as Sam told him harshly, "Your friend Gaffey took a pistol whipping, and Whitey Yates has got a bullet in his hip. I want you to load them both on their horses and take them away from here. And don't be too long about it—understand?"

The other gave him a wordless nod, and Sam dismissed him. He thought no more of the cattle scattered and gone in the timber, or of the bodies of the Denkers. Turning away, he went searching through the trees and across the hoof-torn forest litter of the slope, and so found his brother Mitch

142

lying, face down, where Uncle Rupe's bullet had dumped him. . . .

It was here that the riders from the roundup camp came upon them—Red Steens, Irv Paley, Vic Bonner, and a handful of riders from the different outfits, storming up on lathered horses they'd nearly run into the ground after hearing what Smitty had had to tell them. They discovered Sam Cochran in a stand of twinkling aspen, trimming a couple of saplings he'd laboriously hacked out with his pocket knife. "Putting together a horse drag," he explained tiredly. "Only way I know to get him down from here."

Sam, himself, looked dead on his feet—dirty and unshaven, his face swollen and bruised, and blood on one torn leg of his jeans. But his whole concern seemed to be for his younger brother, lying unconscious on a blanket with his upper body encased in the best crude bandaging Sam had been able to manage. Leora Tabbart, who would not be left behind, came quickly down from her saddle to ask, anxiously, "Sam, how bad is he hurt?"

"I don't know," he said in a leaden voice. "Rupe Denker shot him through the chest. He hasn't spat any blood, so I guess it could have missed the lung."

Vic Bonner demanded, "And the Denkers?"

"They're dead. The men they had with them took off. The herd, too, I guess." He gestured vaguely, indicating the timber of the upward slope. At once Red Steens turned, barking orders; riders from the roundup camp headed for the trees as he sent them after the scattered beef.

Sam was still holding the knife, and one of the poles he'd cut out. Vic Bonner came and took both from his hands, saying, "I can see to this. It's all right. We'll have something rigged and get the boy down out of here, as slick as cow slobbers. You just set and take it easy a minute." Apparently too numb to argue, Sam meekly did as he was told. He wandered a little distance and let himself down with his back against a log, where he could watch the group clustered about the hurt man. He laid his forearms across his knees, his hands dangling limply, and his head drooped and suddenly he began to shake with fatigue and spent nerve.

Irv Paley was there, holding out a bottle. "A slug of this will help, Cochran," he said. Sam looked at the whisky but shook his head. As Paley walked away, Leora came and

143

dropped down on her knees beside Sam Cochran, and laid a hand on his arm.

"Of course you're worried. But he's going to be all right, Sam—I just know he is. We'll take him to T Square, and he'll have the best of everything until he's on his feet again."

"T Square?" Sam looked at her. "Maybe you've forgotten: Me and the kid, we don't belong there any more."

"You belong nowhere else!" she declared vehemently. "Oh, Sam! At least give Mama the chance to admit the mistake she made. After all, it's no use trying to take more than one step at a time. And the thing right now is to get Mitch well again, and—oh, my darling, to make it up for all the wrongs that have been done you!"

She was looking at his battered face. Her eyes held a depth of compassion as she put out a hand to touch the hurt and swollen cheek. Incredulous, Sam fumbled and took the hand in his.

Except for that look, he would scarcely have let himself believe the words he was sure he'd heard her say. As it was, he couldn't answer at once. One part of his mind was absorbing the wonder of it, while another part was already ranging ahead—asking himself just what Jane Tabbart was going to say about it, if and when she learned her daughter was in love with the ranch foreman.

Well, Leora had called it right, of course: You took one step at a time—nobody yet had ever licked all his problems in a single swoop. Sam still had his troubles with Morgan Osgood, assuming the Clawhammer boss survived; and supposing he straightened that out, there would surely be something else. Life wasn't a matter of happy endings, the way the books said. No, it was racing up to each obstacle as it arose, and hoping to live to tackle the next one. And yet, it had its rewards. . . .

Yonder, the drag had been completed, fashioned from aspen poles and blankets and lengths of saddle rope. It had been fastened in place behind Mitch Cochran's horse; now, while someone held the claybank's head to steady it, others were lifting the hurt youth, gently. Sam rose and helped Leora to her feet.

"Let's go home," he said.

144